This is the second novel written by AJ McGillan. As with AJ McGillan's first book, *Mirror Image*, this new book is also based on a dream the author had when she was younger and decided to create a story around it. It has been her dream to write since she was a teenager but only recently was she able to make it a reality.

To my husband, Trevor, for his continued support, and my mother-in-law, Dorothy, whose continued encouragement keeps me writing.

AJ McGillan

THE PRICE OF BLOOD

AUSTIN MACAULEY PUBLISHERS™

LONDON • CAMBRIDGE • NEW YORK • SHARJAH

Ordering Information
Quantity sales: Special discounts are available on quantity purchases by corporations, associations, and others. For details, contact the publisher at the address below.

Publisher's Cataloguing-in-Publication data
McGillan, AJ
The Price of Blood

ISBN 9781643789651 (Paperback)
ISBN 9781643789644 (Hardback)
ISBN 9781645365761 (ePub e-book)

Library of Congress Control Number: 2020908894

www.austinmacauley.com/us

First Published (2020)
Austin Macauley Publishers LLC
40 Wall Street, 28th Floor
New York, N.Y. 10005
U.S.A.

mail-usa@austinmacauley.com
+1 (646) 5125767

Chapter 1

It was windy; tree branches scratched at the window. The pitter patter of rain on the roof was driving me insane. Something felt wrong. On top of James being late, the night felt eerie. Almost like a scene from a horror movie, the part where the scary music played and you knew something was about to happen. Only this was no movie.

Making my way downstairs, I headed to the front door. I lived in this cabin as a child and even after I moved away, I still came to visit. My dad made sure I came back to visit at least every summer. I glanced at the grandfather clock that stood in the hall as it chimed 4 a.m., James was seven hours late. He had been late before, actually quite often, but never this much. I was getting really worried. I picked up the phone. No dial tone. The storm must have knocked out the line. I rummaged in my purse and pulled out my cellphone. I pushed speed dial 1 and waited for the voice to answer on the other end, telling me that he was all right and worked late. Maybe to let me know that he had car trouble and was staying in the city for the night. Instead, I got voicemail.

"Hi, you've reached James Whitfall, of Whitfall and Sons Construction, please call the office during business hours to book an appointment. If you are calling outside of business hours, leave me a message and I'll call you back...*beep*..."

"James. Where are you...? I am very worried. Call me please, as soon as you get this. I don't care what time it is," I said, concerned and hung up the phone. Opening the door, a shiver ran down my back. I was hoping to catch a glimpse of his headlights coming down the road. Nothing. The wind whipped my hair into my eyes and they started tearing up. I closed the door and locked it. I closed my eyes, trying to stop the stinging. Maybe it wasn't just my hair hitting my eyes, maybe it was everything else as well. This was not supposed to happen this way.

James was supposed to be on time. This weekend was supposed to be perfect. Special. A candlelit dinner that didn't happen. A proposal that I knew was coming but he didn't show up, the adding of the wooden chest to the cabin, I thought, as I climbed the stairs.

I laid back down in bed. The cabin has been in my family for four generations, built by my great grandfather. This cabin was a wedding present to his wife on their wedding day. Since then, every generation of my family was proposed to in this cabin and on the day of proposal, they would put a symbol in the house as a reminder of that day. My dad was the one that added the grandfather clock. My grandfather added the dining-room table and chairs. The tradition was to add something handmade. Store-bought didn't count and it had to be made of wood. Nothing metal or technology-based was allowed. Dad said we had to preserve the rustic feeling of the cabin. We had to keep it as much to the original as we could.

Dad needed me to keep up the tradition. Normally, the cabin gets passed down to the son. My dad didn't have any, just two daughters. My older sister moved away when she was 17. I haven't seen her since. She sent a few postcards from Europe, Australia and five months ago, I got one from Mexico. When she took off, Dad looked heartbroken. My sister and I were drifting apart for years before she left, but I never expected her to take off like that. I told Dad not to worry, even if she didn't carry on the tradition, I would. At first, he looked shocked when I first mentioned it. But why wouldn't I do it for him? I knew how much it meant to my dad that the tradition be followed. I think, if Raylene knew what it meant to him and to the legacy of the family, maybe she would have done it. Dad felt it was symbolic, since they had passed on. It was like they could still be there with us, since a piece of what they created had been left there.

Every noise that normally sounded soothing was making me jumpy tonight. The hoot of an owl. The rustling of the leaves in the trees. I pulled the pillow over my face and tried to drown out the noises. It must have worked.

I woke up late the next morning to a crash coming from downstairs. I jumped out of bed and ran to the direction of the noise. Down in the dining room, a large branch had snapped and come through the window and was scraping the side of the china cabinet. It didn't hold any china, just photo albums. I went outside. The branch was still attached to the tree. I wouldn't be able to move it; it was way too big. I would have to pick up something in town to cut it up and some plastic to cover the window until I could replace it. I grabbed my phone and snapped a few pictures of it just in case I had trouble explaining the size or where it was wedged. I went back inside and got dressed; I washed my face and tied my shoulder-length, dirty blonde hair into a loose bun. I had brown eyes, long eyelashes; looking at my eyes now, it was very obvious that I did not get a lot of sleep. I was only 5′1″ and had a petite figure. I never minded being short for the most part now that I was older but every time, I complained about it when I was younger, my dad would only say that the best things come in small packages. I would giggle every time he said it. I never believed him. I rubbed some concealer under my eyes and headed into town.

I grabbed some breakfast at Lucy's and then went to the hardware store.

"Hey, Emily, back in town I see. It has been a long time. How long you here for?" I turned around to come face to face with a tall, handsome man with black hair and green eyes.

"Hi, Adam. Not sure yet, still deciding."

"Bad storm last night, did you do okay out there?"

"A branch came through the window; I need to get it out and cover it up till I can get a new one in." I showed him some of the pictures I had taken earlier.

"I can come out and help…if you like. Dad will be here in a couple hours," he said, handing the phone back to me.

"No, I couldn't do that to you. I am sure you have other stuff to do."

"Dad won't like it if he knew and I didn't help fix it," he said, smiling.

"Well, okay, as long as it is not keeping you from anything." Adam put everything he would need on the counter and rang it up, and I loaded it into my car. I stopped at the liquor store on my way out of town to pick up some beer for him. I figured he would appreciate it after all the work it was going to take to get the tree cut up.

I have known Adam almost all my life. Dad made a joke out of it that during the summers, we were inseparable as kids, I didn't think it was quite that way. I mean, sure, we did some stuff together. It was not like in a small town like this, you could be too choosy on friends; you just hung out with anyone your age pretty much. Even if we were close as kids, it didn't last. We grew apart in high school slowly, having different interests. He was a really big help when my mom died. And then, of course, with me moving to the city, and him being here, it was really hard to stay in touch when we had nothing much in common anymore. We had two very separate lives; he never had the urge to leave. A few years ago, I asked him why he stayed. The only answer he gave was that he was waiting. When I asked him what for, he didn't say anything.

When I got home, I was shocked at the sight of another branch that had gone through the bedroom window. My bedroom. If I had been in there…

It was a rather large log cabin, had three bedrooms. With a beautiful wraparound porch. The living room had a vaulted ceiling and was very spacious. Next to it was the hallway leading to the back of the cabin leading to the bathroom, laundry room, a small storage space along the right side, on the left would lead off into the kitchen. Beside the hallway were the stairs leading upstairs to the three bedrooms. The dining room was beside the stairwell which also had a door leading through to the kitchen. For not having a lot of windows in the cabin, it was still very bright.

Adam showed up a little while later as I was cleaning up the glass inside the cabin. The wind was starting to pick up again.

"Looks like it is going to be another rough one tonight. We should try and get this done quick."

"Yeah and while I was gone, another one came through the bedroom window upstairs as well."

"Oh, okay. Well, I'll bring in the supplies." He did it in a couple of trips. After examining the branch, he realized it was wedged in the corner and wouldn't budge. He climbed onto the roof, and after making sure he was secure and couldn't fall, he started up the chainsaw. When he finally got through, the branch crashed to the bottom, breaking off more of the glass. While Adam was on the roof, he cut through the one going through the bedroom window. I watched as it fell to the ground, and held the ladder as Adam climbed down. I backed away as he stepped off of it.

The wind picked up and knocked the ladder over. I pulled Adam out of the way. He lost his footing and tripped, pulling me down on top of him. We almost made it out of the way but the edge of it hit Adam on the shoulder.

"Sorry, are you okay?" he said, looking me in the eyes.

"Yeah, fine, you broke my fall," I said, lifting myself off of him.

"I think you got the worst of that." He grabbed the ladder and put it away, and brought in the plastic and staples that he didn't grab earlier.

"Okay, so let's try and cut this up smaller, so we can throw it outside in movable pieces and so it doesn't destroy more of your house."

He set up the sawhorse under the branch and I started pulling out the chairs and furniture so they wouldn't be in the way. As he cut off pieces, I threw them out the window. When it got light enough, Adam threw the rest of it out the window. Using a hammer, Adam knocked out the rest of the glass so it wouldn't cut the plastic. I climbed up on a chair, holding up the plastic, as he stapled it on and then he went around and taped the outside edges so the least amount of cold air would come through. When we finished with the dining-room window, we repeated the process with the upstairs window. Adam cleaned up his tools while I continued to sweep up the rest of the glass.

"We are going to have to cut that tree down or at least trim it back to make sure it doesn't happen again," he said.

"Really, you think it will happen again?"

"It might, the tree has gotten pretty tall." Just then, a loud crack rippled above the cabin, followed by a crash. Adam and I ran outside. We no longer had to worry about the tree hitting the house. The wind had blown it over, uprooted the roots and all, and smashed into Adam's truck.

"Oh, no, I am so sorry, Adam."

"Don't be, I'm insured. Although I will be asking to spend the night, 'cause I am not cutting that up tonight to unblock your car." I laughed. His eyes settled on me before looking back at the tree.

"What?"

"Nothing, I…I just like your laugh. I hadn't heard it since…before your dad died."

"Thank you," I said, smiling, "And you are definitely welcome to stay the night." We went back inside; I almost walked into the wooden chest I had made.

"Oh yeah, it was in your car. I figured you wanted it in here," Adam said, seeing the astonishment. Crap. Things were still going wrong. This wasn't supposed to be brought in till after James proposed. I tried calling him again, while Adam hopped in the shower; still, no answer. I grabbed Adam's clothes and threw them in the laundry. He was now a day late. How could he think this is okay, no phone call, no text? I reheated last night's dinner for us and opened a beer for Adam. Wow. Adam came out of the washroom, wrapped in a towel, and it took great effort to not stare. I caught his smirk; I think he noticed me trying not to look.

"Adam. Are you okay, your shoulder?" I asked, seeing the bruise that was forming.

"Yeah, it's nothing. It looks worse than it is."

I felt so bad. The ladder, his truck. All just to help me out. The plastic moved in and out as the wind blew but, so far, was holding up. We ate dinner.

"This is a pretty fancy dinner, I didn't do that much," he said, while eating.

"Oh, it, umm…it was leftovers actually, so I didn't have to do much."

"Were you expecting company?"

"Last night, yes."

"Oh." He looked disappointed, as I saw him glance at the chest that was still by the doorway. After dinner, I went to get cleaned up. The hot water stung my arms. The tree must have scratched me in several places as I was throwing it out the window. I grabbed rubbing alcohol and poured some on the scratches. By the time I got out, Adam had a fire going in the fireplace. I threw his clothes into the dryer and handed Adam another beer as I joined him on the couch.

"Emily, do you remember the summer you spent here when the lake flooded and we couldn't go swimming all summer?"

"How could I forget, all the debris washed up five feet from the house, and Dad was worried that it would continue to flood and we would lose it. That was the summer you and Dad were teaching me how to woodwork."

"Do you remember what you made that summer?"

"A little ballerina music box that didn't spin and had no music," I said, smiling, remembering how hard Adam and I worked on it that summer. Adam pulled it out from behind his back.

"You kept it?" I asked, amazed.

"I told you I would get it finished. It took 15 years but I finally did it," he said, laughing. I opened it and the little wooden ballerina started spinning as I turned the little wooden crank in the back. Even the music worked.

"How?"

"I found a little shop online that made handmade music boxes and asked for instructions." I couldn't believe it, as the little figurine spun in circles. I noticed he also had the box lid engraved on the inside. The door burst open and the box slid out of my hands as I jumped up to run and close it.

Chapter 2

As I was about to close the door, I saw a shadow moving.

"James," I screamed, as I saw him lying on the ground. He was trying to stand back up, but kept stumbling. I ran to help him up and into the cabin. "Are you okay?"

"Yeah, I just fell, had to walk all the way around the tree 'cause I couldn't drive up closer. Wind knocked me off my feet. The weather is crazy."

"Yeah, it started last night. I'm glad you made it; I was worried what happened. You didn't respond to any of my calls or texts."

"I need to get cleaned up, we will talk later," he said, looking at the mud covering the front of his body. He looked at me and smiled.

"Okay," I said, and watched him walk into the washroom.

"So that's the boyfriend I guess?" Adam said, standing up from the couch, heading to the dryer to grab his clothes.

"Yeah, J—"

"James, I caught that when you screamed earlier."

"Adam, I am so sorry. Is the music box okay? I didn't mean to drop it. The door just startled me."

"Yeah, it's fine. No harm done," he said, handing it to me. As the two of us held the box, a moment that seemed like hours passed, and I found myself looking into Adam's eyes. I looked down and he let go of the box. I set it on the fireplace mantle. I heard the change in his voice. I wasn't sure if he was upset about me dropping the box or James showing up. Maybe it was both.

"I should get to bed; I have a lot of work to get done tomorrow."

"Okay, Adam, thank you for your help today, and I am really sorry about your truck." He simply nodded and headed up to the guest bedroom. A short time later, James came out of the washroom. His brown hair slicked back still had water dripping down onto his shoulders. He was the same height as Adam, and had chocolate-brown eyes. His construction jobs kept him buff and gorgeously tanned from working outside all the time.

"So…" I asked.

"So, what?" he asked, grabbing himself a glass of wine.

"Come on, James. You were supposed to be here last night. You didn't call."

"I got busy."

"Busy? James? I am not an idiot. You don't do construction on the weekend, that is your one rule, don't you remember? The company closes at noon on Fridays, unless there is a rush job, and your mom told me there were no rush jobs this weekend," I said, getting angry at his vagueness.

"So, you are checking up on me now?" he said, raising his voice.

"It isn't like that, James. Your mom called me, we talked, but yes, I did ask her about it."

"Why?"

"Seriously, James, you know why, and you weren't answering your phone." By now, both of us were near yelling at each other.

"Don't, you said you forgave me, so why would you bring it up again?"

"Forgiving and forgetting are two very different things."

"You are the one who insisted on this trip up here. I was perfectly fine staying in the city." Had he changed his mind? He acted like…

"You know what, I have had a long day. Dinner from last night is in the fridge. You can take the other guest room tonight. I need time alone and maybe tomorrow we can figure out why you are acting this way."

"I am not acting any way, Emily. I came out here, didn't I? You are blowing everything out of proportion."

"Am I? Then what were you busy with, James? Tell me, so I don't assume the worst." He didn't respond. "Well, then, you can't blame me for thinking–"

"Enough, just go," he fumed. I nodded and headed for the stairs.

"Don't wake Adam when you go to bed, please."

"Adam? Oh, was that the name of the man in the towel. You know that is rich, you blaming me for—"

"James, I have never cheated on you, you have no reason not to trust me. Adam is a friend from the hardware store that helped with the windows today."

"Windows?"

"Wow. Yes, windows, they are missing, plastic is up," I said, pointing to the plastic.

"Oh, right. Must have been a hell of a wind up here."

"Yeah."

"Okay, so he helped you out. Why is he still here? And why was he not dressed?"

"His clothes were dirty, and he didn't have a spare set, so he was in a towel while I washed his clothes. And, James, how much have you been drinking? The tree in the front yard fell over and crushed his truck. You complained about having to walk around it, remember? My car is blocked in, we are going to cut it up tomorrow."

"Oh, I can drive him back if he wants."

"James, just leave it alone. You have been drinking and with how oblivious you are, I don't want you driving, let alone having someone with you. Besides, he has already gone to bed." James was not like himself. I didn't know what was wrong or, why he was behaving this way, but he was more volatile than normal. I honestly didn't know if this romantic weekend was going to be romantic; I didn't know if he was going to propose anymore. I pushed it out of my thoughts and climbed the stairs. I saw Adam at the end of the hall. He had heard everything.

"Sorry you had to hear that," I said, embarrassed. "Good night." Shutting my room door and locking it, I had no intention of letting James in here tonight. I looked at the plastic that covered the window, it looked like the plastic was breathing. It was creepy. I closed my eyes and took a deep breath. Could things get any worse? I jumped when I heard a soft knock on my door. I unlocked it and opened it, expecting to see James coming to apologize. There was no one there. Puzzled, I closed the door. I turned out the light and crawled into bed. Maybe it was in my head. Maybe I needed James to come and apologize. Just so I didn't have all the weird thoughts going on in my head. I told him directly about Adam, answered all of his questions, and he dodged my question of why he was late. And sure enough, as I tried to sleep, the thoughts did come. Images of the fights we had before when I found out he had been cheating on me. I had never met her but knew of her. Was this girl the same one or was she a new girl? The harder I tried not to think about it, the more the images came. Blondes at first, then remembered him admitting he preferred redheads; I even tried dying my hair red a couple times for him, but I really did not look good with red hair. It was driving me crazy. All he had to do was say it was not a woman, and I would have believed him.

Needless to say, I did not get much sleep. I woke up tired and went to make coffee.

"Morning," Adam said, coming into the kitchen.

"Oh, morning, Adam," I said, choking down the coffee. I almost had forgotten that he was here; I usually didn't have company over when I stayed here. Adam stared at me, looking me up and down. Even in a tank top and shorts, when Adam looked at me, I felt naked. "I should go get dressed."

"You are dressed," he said, smiling. He had a nice smile.

"I am not wearing this to clean up the mess outside," I said quickly, not wanting him to notice I was looking at him longer that I should have been. *Emily, stop it, you are about to be engaged and yes, Adam is pleasing to look at, but...crap.* His smile got bigger, almost as if he knew I was thinking about him.

"Ah, yes. You would get a lot more scratched up if you wear that." I returned a little while later to find Adam making eggs. He handed me a plate.

"Emily, what on earth is going on out there?" I heard a female voice come through the kitchen doorway.

"Ray, is that you?" I leapt off my seat and ran out of the kitchen. I saw her put down a bag and we squealed at seeing each other. I had a healthy self-esteem, but around my sister, if guys were around, I didn't exist. She was 5'8" with long, wavy, strawberry-blonde hair, amazing, sparkling, hazel eyes.

"How long has it been?"

"12 years since you left," I replied.

"12 years, has it really been that long?"

"Yeah, why...what...?"

"Oh, well, I remembered Dad insisting on tradition, and since I got your letter two years ago saying he was gone, I decided that he was right. If he is not here in person, it feels right that it gets done here."

"Ray, does this mean you are getting married?"

"Unofficially, yes. Officially, I have to wait to be asked," she said, looking out at the man approaching with bags in hand. He was a couple inches taller than her, had average features, not particularly muscular, but still looked strong. He had blonde hair cut military style and blue eyes.

"I am so glad you are here, Emily, and you can enjoy this with us. I want to make sure everything is perfect. I want to make Dad happy. I know we never saw eye-to-eye, but I need to do this for him. Ben agrees."

"Ben, is that his name?"

"Yes," she said, beaming, as he climbed the stairs on the porch and set the bags down.

"Well, that is some obstacle course you have out there," he said, offering his hand. "I'm Ben."

"Emily," I said, shaking his outstretched hand.

"Do you need any help with anything?" Adam asked, coming out of the kitchen.

"Adam, holy crap, you are looking fine. Are you two...?" Raylene said excitedly, as she ran up to him and gave him a hug. James also was watching and hearing Raylene's outburst.

"No," I said quickly, catching James's disapproving look from the top of the stairwell. "He came to help with the storm and got stuck here when the tree crushed his truck."

"Oh, Adam, I am so sorry, that sounds like shitty luck," she said.

16

"Depends on how you look at it, I guess," he said, looking at me, then back to her.

"This is the most excitement this town has had in a while." Raylene started laughing and then saw James coming down the stairs. Adam and Ben went to get the last of their bags from the car.

"Do you really have to make so much noise so early in the morning?" he said, reaching the bottom of the stairs.

I could still smell the liquor in his breath; he must have switched to harder alcohol after I went to bed. And by his mood, he was definitely hung-over.

"James, we have company. Please, at least pretend to be nice," I whispered, and pushed him toward the kitchen. He grunted but complied. I could tell Raylene overheard, but acted as if she didn't, which I was very grateful for. As I turned out to look at Ben and Adam, Ben fell face first into the mud. I really didn't want to laugh but I couldn't help it. Raylene ran to him to help him up, and landed on her butt trying to get to him, which made me laugh harder. When everyone made it into the cabin, we surveyed the mud everywhere.

"Ben, we should hop in the shower and minimize some of this mess," she said, grabbing his hand with a seductive smile.

"Yes, but first," he said, dropping to a knee, "I think you have made me wait long enough. Raylene, will you marry me?"

"Yes, but if you think I am kissing you with all that mud on you, you are crazy," she said teasingly.

"That's okay, you don't have to kiss me, I'll kiss you," he said, and grabbed her around the waist, pulling her in for a kiss.

"That was the messiest proposal I have ever seen. Literally. But your kids are going to love the story," Adam said, smiling. They stepped away from each other and grinned.

"Ben never does things the normal way. It is only one of the reasons I love him."

She unzipped a duffel bag and pulled out two wooden picture frames with intricate filigree designs etched into them. One had a picture of her and Ben. The other, of Mom and Dad.

"So how long are you going to stay?" Raylene asked me, putting the frames on the fireplace mantle, one on either side of the music box. I saw her looking at it thoughtfully and then noticing the chest still by the door but she didn't say anything.

"I hadn't planned on anything specific, I needed...I don't know what exactly but I am hoping time out here will help clarify. How 'bout you? What date were you looking at?"

"Well, since it is official now, we were not planning to wait too long, maybe a few weeks."

"I can do that; I was actually going to try and spend the whole summer this year. Trying to find some inspiration, I guess." I caught Adam looking at me but turned away when James came back out of the kitchen.

"Hi," Raylene said, looking at James.

"Oh, sorry, umm…James, this is my sister, Raylene, and her fiancé, Ben, and this is Adam." His eyes avoided Raylene and briefly landed on Ben but was more focused on Adam.

"Emily, should we get started?" Adam asked, seeing that the situation was getting a bit awkward.

"Yeah, coming." I hurried after Adam. He pried open the passenger-side door after bending back a few branches and handed me a pair of work gloves. "Will the little chainsaw I bought do something this big?"

"Maybe. It isn't supposed to but unless you want me to call Rick and see when he can come out."

"Rick?"

"Yeah, umm, maybe you don't remember, you and he never really got along. But I can call him if you want."

"Oh, well, we can try to do what we can, I guess, at least clean up the smaller stuff and if we can't do the bigger ones, we can call him later."

"Or we could call and see if he even has time. If this happened all over town, we might be waiting a while anyway. But we definitely can start with the trimming."

"Sure, that sounds good." Adam and I started at the base of the tree and worked our way up, removing the branches off the tree. A lot of them were huge, so had to cut them a few times to make it more manageable. I looked at the roots and a puzzled look must have been on my face because Adam was looking at me curiously.

"What's that look for?"

"It doesn't make sense. This tree is huge, the roots seem so strong. I realize the wind was really bad yesterday, but even so, how could it have knocked a tree over with roots like that?" I said, pointing to the base of the tree.

"Maybe the roots were rotted on the inside or the ground was loosened by the lake. There could have been a number of reasons for this, Emily. I, for one, am never questioning what nature is capable of." I nodded, even though I couldn't fully agree with his reasoning. The roots didn't look rotten, and the lake was regular level for this time of year.

By noon, Raylene and Ben joined us, with big smiles on their faces and all cleaned up. I smiled at them; they looked so cute and in love. Meanwhile,

18

James was standing in the doorway, not making any attempt to help. Just watched us working. I sighed and shook my head but stopped when I saw Adam looking. He saw James by the doorway too.

"You good?" he asked.

"Yeah, fine." My perfect weekend of getting engaged to a man I thought I loved was turning into a nightmare with a man who I barely recognized. Where was the James I loved? The one I wanted to marry? But Raylene was engaged now, and whatever I thought was going to happen with James could wait till my sister was happily married. My drama with James could wait till after, and as far as his attitude since he got here, it told me he could wait till after the summer. He was fine when he showed up and then suddenly changed. Was he acting this way because of Adam?

"So, Rick will be here in an hour or so." I saw Adam watching James as he continued to eat the plate of food that he made for me, that I didn't get to eat because I was distracted when Raylene showed up. This was starting to feel awkward. James not caring enough when he should be, and Adam caring too much when he shouldn't be. This was almost like a freaky Friday moment. Adam and I worked in silence, Ben and Raylene half worked, half played. We were mostly done when Rick showed up. He didn't speak to me but went straight up to Adam and started barking orders at him. Ben and Raylene got ordered to sort the piles for wood for the fireplace that was already small enough, and the wood that needed to be set aside for being chopped into firewood, and then the branches that we couldn't use at all and would be burned. I was told to stay out of the way. Now I remembered why I didn't like Rick. Rick was Adam's uncle and ever since I was little, I remembered him being rude and arrogant. He was a couple inches shorter than Adam, black hair, brown eyes, and looked really good for his age. He must have been nearing 60, but still looked as if he was in his 40s. I remembered several conversations that my mom had with him that ended up with her in tears. Though I didn't know the content of the conversations, Mom warned me to stay away from him, that he wasn't nice. I went to go pick up the glass that had fallen to the outside of the house.

Chapter 3

"So you wanna tell me what's going on?" Raylene said, coming up to me.

"With what?"

"The two guys who seem to be throwing daggers by the way they are looking at each other," she said, and bent down to pick up the glass with me.

"Honestly, I have no idea. Adam, we have known since we were kids and he has never acted this way."

"Could it be because you have never brought a guy here before?" I rolled my eyes at her, but something made me scour my memories, and she was right. I hadn't ever brought a guy here before. Well, actually, I did bring James a few times before, but we didn't go into town, so Adam probably didn't know about those times.

"I don't think it is that," I said, but both of us knew I didn't believe it as much as I thought I did.

"All right, and what is the story with man number two?"

"Again, no idea. He was supposed to be here Friday, shows up Saturday night. Refused to give me a reason. Has been moody since he got here." I decided to leave out the proposal part because if it wasn't for his meddling mother, I wouldn't have known he was planning to do it this weekend.

"It's okay, you can tell me the rest later."

"What? How did you know…?"

"We might not have seen each other for a while, but you still make that same face."

"What face?"

"The same face you made when you knew Jimmy Richt was cheating on me in high school, and didn't know how to tell me."

"Fine, I'll tell you later. So, tell me about you."

"That is also a later thing to discuss," she said, turning away.

"What's—ouch," I screamed. I moved too quickly with one of the larger pieces of glass when I was watching Raylene instead of what I was doing, and I sliced my hand, which made me drop it, as well as the other pieces I was holding, and it hit my arm and leg as well.

"Adam." Raylene got up and ran to get him. She quickly explained what happened and he came running. Raylene was squeamish at the sight of blood, so she kept her distance, and even though I could walk, Adam insisted on carrying me to the bathroom. The only one that was deep was the one on my hand, but it didn't need stitches. Adam cleaned the wounds and bandaged them up.

"There you go, all done," he said, smiling at me.

"You have him eating out of the palm of your hand, what did you promise him for his services?" James said, beer in hand, peering through the bathroom door, glaring at Adam and me. I couldn't believe him.

"He was just helping me, James, there is nothing going on between us," I said, embarrassed, as Adam was witnessing the scene. What was wrong with him? Or was he always this way, and because I never went anywhere except for work or shopping, he didn't feel the need to bring this side of himself out? Was he jealous of Adam? Could he really think I would cheat on him?

"James, what is wrong with you? You have been drinking since you got here, which I have never seen you do. You have been moody and rude."

"Don't change the subject. No guy is this nice without getting something in return. What is he getting out of this?"

"I should get back to the guys," Adam said awkwardly, brushing past James.

"Yeah, I still have work to do as well," I said, trying to follow after him.

"No, you are not going anywhere," he said, shoving me backward as I exited the bathroom. "You and I need to talk."

"Hey, man, what is your deal?" Adam said, watching the situation unfold. "Emily, come on." He took up a defensive stance beside me incase James tried to grab me again.

"You stay out of this."

"James, enough, we will talk when you sober up," I said, disgusted, and at this point, I was beginning to question what I ever saw in him. Could I really have been that wrong about him to never see this side of him? "I will help you back to bed."

"Yeah," he said, perking up, "let's go to bed." I didn't argue with him. He can think I will join him all he wants if it will help me get him into bed easier. I struggled getting him upstairs. For some reason, he felt me helping him up the stairs meant throw all your body weight on me. I got him into bed and he grabbed at me, trying to kiss me. He got a hold of my shirt and tried to pull me onto the bed with him.

"James, NO. You sober up and then we need to talk."

"Bah, I'm fine, you just need to make me feel better."

"No, when you are acting more like yourself again, we can talk."

"Come on, Emily, quit playing hard to get. You knew what was going to happen this weekend when you invited me to a very private, secluded cabin for the whole weekend."

"With the way you have been acting, you bet I can. You have done shit to make me want to do anything with you."

"Come on, since when have you ever needed me to do the seduction thing to get you in the mood?" He was right. I was usually pretty easy to get into bed, but that was when he was acting normal. This was not him.

"Since you started acting like an ass." He grabbed at my shirt again, ripping the bottom of it. "James. Stop. Sleep off whatever is going on with you." He finally let go and passed out. I closed the door behind me.

"Did he...?" Raylene asked when she saw my shirt.

"No, his hand got caught in my shirt when I was laying him down."

"You should change before Adam sees and gets madder than he already seems to be," she said.

"You think he is mad?"

"Maybe mad isn't the right word, but you wouldn't want to provoke more...Crap, too late." And just as Raylene had said, it did provoke a reaction out of Adam.

"No, Adam, don't. He didn't do anything," I said, putting my hands on his chest to keep him from going into the room. "He didn't mean to; he is just not himself right now."

"Fine, I will wait till he is himself."

"No, you won't do anything, even when he is himself. Please just leave this alone." He looked at me, and then at the door to James's room. His eyes shifted to my hands that were still on his chest. He took a step back, nodded, and went back outside. The look on Adam's face scared me. I had never seen him look that intense. I changed my shirt and went back to cleaning up the glass. Raylene and I finally got it all into the garbage bin. There were still glass pieces on the roof, but I left them there. I could clean it up when we put the window in.

"Ray, is it just me, or is everyone acting strange?"

"Emily, I can't answer that. I don't know the men that well. And I haven't seen you in years. As for Ben and I, we seem to be the same."

"You know, that feels weird too. You and I haven't talked in years, and you being here feels like you never left." She thought for a moment, taking in the last words that I said.

"Okay, that, I have to agree with. It does feel like I have been here the whole time, even though I know I haven't."

"Okay, so what made you decide on picture frames for the cabin?"

"I was never good at wood stuff, not like you."

"Honestly, if you gave it a shot, you might have been. You were always distracted with Michael Keller during that class, remember?" She grinned.

"Okay, so maybe I could have been a little better. But honestly, it is not my thing. Just something that I was supposed to do."

"So, Ray, why did you leave?"

"At the time, I couldn't stay. There were so many reasons, but I had to leave, or I would have gone crazy. Literally."

"But for 12 years, you didn't even come back once."

"I know, and for a while, I needed to stay away. I was going through so much and couldn't talk about it. I thought staying away would help, not being around you and Dad and this cabin," she said, looking around.

"If you ever want to tell me, I am willing to listen. I always would have been willing to listen."

"Sure, Emily, I know that. Maybe one day, but not right now," she said, avoiding eye contact. She walked away, heading toward Ben. I sat perched on the railing of the porch. My arm and hand still stinging. The one on my leg was easier to ignore.

The sun was shining brightly today. It was hard to believe the previous days were so bad. But looking across the lake, I saw more bad weather moving in. I went to go find Raylene.

"Think you can take me into town later today? I need to get the new windows ordered and get some more food since we have a fuller house than I expected."

"Yeah, sure, but Ben was going to take me on a picnic at the place where we went as kids, the spot at the lake."

"Right, the place where you nearly gave me a heart attack, making me think you drowned?"

"Yeah, that was stupid of me, but at the time, I thought it was funny. Maybe I could take you in tomorrow, we might be gone most of the afternoon."

"Okay, I have to measure the windows and stuff anyway." I saw Adam by his truck. It looked worse now that the tree was off of it. Not only was the truck totaled, but the number of tools and equipment in the truck that were now useless and would have to be replaced.

"Adam, I am so sorry. Look at all your stuff."

"Well, Emily, that is just it," he said, looking me in the eyes. "It is just stuff; it can be replaced. At least no one got hurt."

"Ray is going to drive me into town tomorrow to get the windows ordered. Could I get your help one last time before you leave?"

"Leave?" he asked. He looked almost hurt that I would say that.

"Well, you don't have to, I just thought…with Rick…You know what, never mind. You can stay as long as you would like."

"I would like to stay…at least till James is normal. To use your words. But what did you need help with?"

"Oh, right. I need to get the windows ordered, so I have to get the opening measured."

"Sure, no problem." We walked into the cabin together. Maybe Raylene was right. Maybe Adam was jealous. Me mentioning him leaving seemed to surprise him. No, he was just concerned, with the way James was acting. Hell, even I was concerned. I mean, Adam has known me since we were kids. Why wouldn't he want to make sure I was okay? It is not like James was showing the best side of him.

"Adam, I've got most of this done. Ben said he would sort the rest of it," Rick said.

"Thanks, Rick," Adam replied.

"I will be in town tomorrow to settle the bill," I replied.

"Sure, I will have my wife keep it at the office for you." *That is sweet.* I thought to myself. His wife as his secretary. The two men nodded at each other and Rick left.

"Thank you for keeping the peace," Adam said.

"Honestly, I don't even remember him, what is it that we don't get along about?" I pretended not to remember Rick. Adam was being really sweet in helping me, last thing I wanted to do was start insulting his family in front of him.

"Let's not open that can of worms. So, shall we get started?" Adam said. We got the two windows measured, then went down to make some dinner.

"So, is your life always this intense?" Adam asked. I smirked.

"Up until this weekend, I would call my life boring routine. I was going to ask you the same thing."

"No, this is definitely not normally part of my day. My days consist of taking care of the shop, how 'bout you, what's your routine like?"

"My work, reading, lots of movies."

"What do you do for work these days? Last time we talked about jobs, you were still working at that fast-food place, and that was almost ten years ago?"

"What is this, are we playing 20 questions?"

"Hey, you know what I do for work."

"I guess it is only fair then. I am a freelance photographer. Mostly do weddings, but I have done a few commissions for art galleries. They really like the scenic ones that I take when I come out here."

24

"Do you like it?"

"I get to travel every now and then, so it is nice, and I get to pick the jobs I want to take on, so the freedom to do that is a bonus."

"So how long are you here for?"

"Well, at least for the summer. Wanted to take some time off, I haven't really taken a vacation in a while. The last couple years, I haven't been able to stay out here long when I came." Remembering when Dad passed away, I— "What about you? Haven't you ever wanted to take time off, get away from the routine?" I asked, not wanting to think about that right now.

"Honestly, no, not really." I looked at him skeptically. "You ever wonder where you would be today, if you had never left?"

"Maybe, sometimes. The quiet out here would be nice, but I would not get half the amount of work out here that I do in the city, and would probably not be able to make a living off of it and support myself with it. This town is too small."

"Well, I saw the chest out there. If you need some extra money, you could always start up a side business building stuff. You already know that people around here love that kind of stuff, and the tourists love it even more. You know the quaint little town and it's do-it-yourself town folk." We laughed.

"Yes, but most of the people out here, like you said, do it themselves. They would not buy something they can make themselves just as easily."

"Are you still here? Isn't the shit moved yet?" James said, stumbling into the kitchen.

"James, stop. Whatever is wrong with you, you need to stop."

"There is nothing wrong with me."

"Adam is welcome to stay as long as he needs to 'cause his truck is still totaled. And, James, you can head back to the city as soon as you can drive. I don't want you here anymore."

"No, I drove all the way out here for you, you owe me," he said, grabbing me hard by the arm.

"I owe you nothing. I invited you here; I did not force you. You came on your own and have been an ass since." I pulled my arm free from his grasp.

"Emily." I looked at him and didn't say anything.

"Adam, can you drive me into town please? I need to get more groceries and hopefully James will be gone by the time we get back," I said, giving him a pointed look.

"We? You are bringing him back?" James said, fuming.

"Yes," I said, and pushed past him. Adam followed me out.

"Do you think he will actually leave?" Adam asked on the drive to town.

"I don't know," I said.

I thought I knew him. Besides him cheating on me, he was kind, he would ask what I thought about. We talked. Whatever was happening this weekend with him was a side of him I have never seen. I knew we were drifting apart the last year or so, since he cheated on me, but I was hoping, with the conversations with his mom, that we were moving past it, that we could get back to normal. We had been slowly working on building back the trust and up till now, I could see myself with him. Our lives may not have been perfect, but after seeing him this weekend, I was not so sure anymore. Adam saw the worried look on my face and didn't ask anything else.

We couldn't order the windows; the store was closed. I watched as Adam interacted with the people in town. Everyone was on a first-name basis. They knew about each other and their families; it was weird to think that people could know so much about each other. If my neighbors knew that much about me in the city, I would consider them nosy. Here, it was normal. They seemed to care about each other, and not just superficially. If they asked how you were, they actually really wanted to know. Adam directed me to Rick's office. His wife was just printing out the bill, which I paid. She was a very talkative woman. It was very hard to leave. I did what I could to not be rude. Adam finally stepped in and said we had more stuff to do before it got too late. She understood and let us leave.

He drove us to the gas station which was the location of the only tow truck in town, and arranged for his truck to be towed to his place when they had the time. Then, he drove to the grocery store and we grabbed food.

"So, don't take this the wrong way, but I would like to compensate you for some of the damage to your truck. I feel really bad."

"No, it is insured. It is fine, you don't have to."

"Well, then for your time, missing work, and helping me out so much."

"I was glad I could be there, so you don't need to pay me for that. Which reminds me, we should stop at the pharmacy on the way back to your place. With how many cuts and scrapes you have been getting, you need more supplies," he said, laughing. I smiled. He was not wrong. The bandages he put on me earlier needed changing. We bought a few stuff at the pharmacy and then headed back to the cabin.

"So, why did you ask me to do the driving?" Adam finally asked as we approached home.

"A couple of reasons. First, my hand hurts like hell, and gripping a steering wheel might not be the best thing for it. And second, I didn't think I should leave you in the house with James in his current condition."

"Both excellent reasons," he said, smiling.

Adam helped me unload the groceries from the car. We found Ben and Ray in the kitchen. They attacked the groceries when we brought them in. I guess they were hungry.

"We can make dinner, you guys relax." We brought in the rest of the food and let them put it away. James's car was still here. I hadn't seen him, but he was obviously still around.

"Come on, I'll get your bandages changed while we wait." I headed out to the porch.

"Might as well make use of the last of the light. I don't get to do this in the city. Well, I guess I do, but it is not nearly the same thing." The town was nestled in the mountains, about four hours from the city. Even in the middle of the summer, the nights cooled down enough to need the fireplace year-round. It was ideal and very picturesque. I have sold so many photographs of this place. Between the town and the lakes nearby, if you didn't mind the cold, it was ideal for artists which this town got their fair share of all year.

There were two lakes. One was right next to my family's cabin, the other was on the far end of town. Just as the road headed down the mountain, the lake stopped abruptly There may have been a waterfall at some point, but unless the lake overflowed, no one got to see it anymore. It was more of a cliff face now. Being on the far end of town, we didn't get that many tourists or visitors on this end. The other lake got a lot more traffic, being closer to town. I couldn't help but look out over the landscape and rushed inside to get my camera. I took a few pictures and noticed Adam watching me.

"You really have the best view of the sunsets, with the lake there, definitely don't see the same ones at my place." We sat down on the bench. I noticed the weather would not stay nice long. "Don't worry, it is still a couple hours away. Enjoy it." He was right, no need to worry about what was coming. We would deal with it when it got here.

"Adam, why are you helping me?"

"Because you need it."

"But—"

"Look, I don't know how you do things in the city, or what kind of friends you have. But people around here, we help people who need it, even Rick. I know you only are here to visit when you come, but we all know your family. Your grandpa delivered at least one, if not more, child in each of the families that live around here. I know that Raylene left, and you, when you could. The death of your mother was hard on you guys, and leaving seemed like it was better for you, so don't take this the wrong way, but we looked out for your dad after you left. He helped us out a lot to keep himself busy, and people in this town don't forget stuff like that." My eyes started tearing up, listening to him talk about my family.

"We should probably stock up on the wood in the house, it is probably going to get very wet and cold tonight," I said, glancing at the clouds rolling in, trying to take my mind off how much I missed my dad. Adam's hand lingered on mine as he finished re-bandaging it. I took a few more pictures as the clouds came rolling in. Sometimes, beauty could be found in the storm.

A little while later, Ben called us for dinner. James hadn't made an appearance all night. Maybe he was still trying to cool off from whatever was going on with him. During dinner, Raylene and Ben told us about some of the places they traveled to. The conversation was light and fun.

"So how did you two meet?" Adam asked.

"I started working at a farm in Mexico for extra cash, while I was figuring out where to go next," Raylene said.

"And I was just about to leave 'cause my vacation was almost up. I think I had four days left before heading to my next destination, but when I saw her, we got talking. We talked for hours and the next day, I cancelled my plans, stayed on for as long as she worked there, and pretty much have been following her ever since," he said, smiling at her. He took her hand and kissed the top of it.

"You are so sweet, you know that?" She leaned in and kissed him.

"Wow, that is amazing," I said, smiling, making sure they still knew there were other people in the room.

After dinner, I went to go do the dishes while Adam made a fire.

"Have I really been an ass all weekend?" James asked. He was standing in the shadows of the kitchen. He sounded normal again.

"Yes, James. I just want to know what is wrong. You have been weird all weekend. I have never seen you like this."

"It's him, he wants you," he said bitterly.

"Don't blame this on Adam. He and I have known each other since we were kids. And your attitude started before you got here. So, let's start there. Why were you late?"

He got a faint look of confusion on his face and ignored my question.

"Don't you see it? The hunger," his voice started sounding weird again.

"James, you are scaring me, what's wrong?" He moved out of the shadows; his eyes all bloodshot. He almost looked like he didn't recognize his own name when I talked to him.

"You need to send him away. He is not good for you."

"James, I am not dating him, I am dating you. This jealousy thing needs to stop."

"He wants you; I can feel it." For a moment, he sounded scared and more like himself. Then, he was back to being creepy. He started yelling, grabbed my shoulders, and started shaking me. "Send him away." He kept repeating himself over and over again.

I must have been screaming because the next thing I knew, Ben and Adam were wrestling James away from me. Raylene took me out of the room. She came back a little while later and handed me a glass of wine. I sipped it as I watched the flames in the fireplace.

"How is he?"

"They have him in the bedroom. But there is something wrong with him." Suddenly, there was banging on the bedroom door upstairs. Adam was rushing down the stairs, he grabbed something and ran back up. There was more banging and shouting. And then nothing.

Even though things were now silent, it still frightened me. Raylene was watching me. I was shaking.

"Emily, I definitely believe you. I think there is something very wrong with James. I know I haven't been around, but you would never date a guy who acted like that on a regular basis."

"Raylene, come on, let's leave them," Ben said, coming down the stairs, with Adam trailing after. Raylene stood up and left with Ben into the kitchen. Adam took the spot on the couch beside me.

"Is he okay?" I asked, scared what the answer might be.

"I gave him a sedative, and Ben had to tie him to the bed." I must have had a look of horror on my face, because he quickly added, "We didn't want him to hurt anyone." I nodded. I might not have liked the idea, but I understood why they did it. "I am going to call the doctor; we will see if maybe he can tell us what is wrong with him." I nodded again.

"Wait, where did you get the sedatives?"

"I got some when we were at the pharmacy today. I was worried you might have some trouble sleeping with everything that is going on. It was only in case you needed it." Adam tried the landline; it was still out of order. He stepped out on the porch and called the doctor. He came back in a few seconds later.

"Hopefully he got what I was saying. With the storm, the reception wasn't great. How are you doing?"

"This weekend was supposed to go so differently, time up here is supposed to be relaxing, less stressful than the city," I said, laughing. "This has been anything but."

"Do you regret coming here?" he asked. I thought about the question.

"No," I finally said. "Even though he is not himself, it is a good thing that I saw this side of him before…Anyway, it is good to know, I needed to know that he was capable of acting this way. And I am really glad to see Ray and to meet Ben. I am also really glad you are here. I don't know what would have happened if you hadn't been here," I said, looking up at him, the flames from the fire lighting up his face. Even though James was acting crazy right now, I finally saw what he was seeing. Adam did have an intense look in his eyes when he looked at me. And for a moment, it scared me. But just as quickly as the moment came, it also faded. He has been helping me, protecting me. Did he know James would act this crazy? No, that was ridiculous. Now I was starting to think crazy.

"Honestly, I am not sure if me being here has helped or made things worse. He doesn't seem to like me being here. Anyway, I think I should give the bedroom to the happy couple. Do you have extra blankets? I can take the couch."

"Umm, yeah," I said, pulling myself out of my thoughts. I set my wine down and went to the linen closet on the second floor to grab him blankets. I found myself pausing and looking down the hall to the room they put James in. A crack of thunder above the cabin made me jump. I heard the rain pelt down onto the roof. I returned to Adam and handed him a pillow and blanket.

"Emily, I am sorry that this isn't the weekend you were hoping for."

"Yeah, me too. I am sorry about the way James is acting toward you. He has never done anything like this before."

"Not a big deal, I guess I should feel flattered that he finds me a threat," he said with a smirk.

"You would," I said, laughing. "So, if the doctor understood you, when do think he should be here?"

"He should be here soon. He is actually not far from here. He lives in McKinnley's old place. They moved to the city and he looks after it for them."

"Must be nice that they don't have to worry about the place. I worry about this place sometimes when I am in the city. Coming out here once a year doesn't feel like it is often enough. Especially lately. It is weird, even with everything that has happened in the last couple days, it is still peaceful here."

"You don't need to worry about the place. Your family built it strong."

"Yeah. It hasn't needed a whole lot of maintenance, which is quite surprising. I'm just glad I was here for this storm. I can't imagine what damage could have happened if it would have been left alone for who knows how long until I got to visit again."

"I guess I should confess that I may have been looking in on the place for you from time to time."

"Adam, that is surprising and really sweet."

"I don't know about surprising, I told you, your family has done a lot for this town, but I will accept you calling me sweet." I smiled and gave him a little shove.

"You always did like the compliments."

"It is better hearing them from someone else than me looking in the mirror to do it." We both laughed. A couple minutes later, Adam got up to go answer the door. With the storm outside, I didn't even hear anyone knocking. The storm outside was getting worse. Adam showed the doctor to the room James was sleeping in. I refused to go see him like that. I didn't want to see him tied up. Well, not for this reason anyway. We had tried it for other reasons, I thought to myself. I couldn't help but smile. It was actually really embarrassing. I remember that was the day I had met James's mom.

I also think that was the day James revoked his mom's key to his house. At least, the redeeming factor that it was James tied up and not me. I had the chance to wrap a sheet around me before she opened the door. She told me later that even though she walked in on us, she still liked me right away. She thought it was funny that I would leave him naked instead of giving the sheet to him. She and I got along well, which apparently wasn't the case with a lot of James's girlfriends.

"Hey, Emily, we are heading to bed. Are you going to be okay?" Raylene called, heading up the stairs, snapping me out of my thoughts.

"Yeah, I'll be fine. The doctor is with James."

"Hopefully he can help him. Umm, which room should we take?"

"Take mine, you know which one." Raylene nodded and grabbed Ben's hand.

"Goodnight," he called to me, as Raylene pulled at him lightly to follow. I still couldn't believe how, after all this time, it felt like she had never been gone. With everything that has been going on, I was really happy that she was home again. That she was doing this to make Dad happy. That she cared.

I was so entranced by the fire that I didn't notice when Adam came down the stairs. He tapped me on the shoulder. I gasped so hard, it made me cough.

"Sorry, I called, you must have not heard me."

"No, I didn't. It's okay," I said. "I have been a little jumpy the last couple days. Doctor find anything?"

"James has a high fever. Doc says he needs to stay in bed. Moving him could make it worse."

"Could that be what is making him act...the way he is?" I asked, trying to put it nicely.

31

"He is not sure. He says to let the fever break and keep a close eye on him and see if he gets better. He will be by tomorrow to check on him." I nodded. "Oh, and he did say it might be a wise precaution to keep him tied up, since he was showing signs of violence, to keep everyone else safe."

"Okay. Ray and Ben took my room, so you can still keep the bedroom. I will keep an eye on James tonight."

He nodded and returned upstairs. I went to the kitchen and wet some dishcloths and threw them in the freezer.

"Thank you for coming, even with the weather the way it is," I said, when the doctor came down.

"Not a problem. I am glad you called. He is in bad shape. Keep him warm. He is going to say he is hot and cold at the same time. He is going to be delirious, might say strange things. I have given him some medication to help him sleep, but I don't think it will last long. The fever will burn it out of his system quick. Adam says he has some sedatives left, and although I don't recommend giving him any, if he gets too bad, you may need to give him some."

"Okay."

"Adam also tells me you were hurt this morning. Would you like me to look at it?"

"It should be fine, Adam said they weren't bad."

"Forgive me, but Adam is not a doctor." He took the wrappings off the three wounds, cleaned them again for me, and re-dressed them.

"So was I right, Doc?" Adam said, coming down the stairs.

"You did all right; they don't look that serious. The one on your hand, you may have to watch closely, has more of a chance of getting infected."

"I will. Thank you, Doctor." Adam saw him out. They talked for a couple minutes and then he came back inside.

"He thinks James will get better soon. The fever was caught in time."

"That's good. I should probably call his mom, since he won't be able to head back into the city. She can tell his dad he won't be back at work for a bit."

"Well, if you will be okay, I think I will head to bed. It has been a long day."

"Yeah, it has."

"If you need me…for anything, don't hesitate to wake me," he said grabbing my hands. He emphasized the 'for anything.'

"Thank you, Adam. And I know I have said it before, but you have been really sweet to help out so much this weekend. Your parents must be proud to have a son like you," I said, giving him a kiss on the cheek. "And you are going to make a great husband one day to a lucky girl." Wait, why did I just do that?

"Sometimes, I am not so sure," he said, looking away, embarrassed. "My dad and I haven't been seeing eye-to-eye lately. I am not sure if he is proud of me anymore. But all the rest, I can agree with," he said, laughing. I laughed with him.

"Well, get some sleep," I said, and watched as he went upstairs. *What was wrong with me?* My boyfriend, and supposed-to-be-soon-fiancé, was upstairs, sick in bed, and I was flirting with another man. This was not me. I was not normally like this. Maybe I was getting sick too. Or maybe I was so needing attention this weekend and James was clearly...*Oh, stop making excuses*, I thought. Shaking myself out of my thoughts.

I grabbed the cold cloths and a bowl of ice water, then headed up to James. He was wrapped up tight in the blanket and was sound asleep. I set the bowl down beside the bed and set one of the cloths on his forehead. He should be asleep for a little while yet. I headed back downstairs and called his mother.

"Emily, it is really late. What's wrong?"

"It's James, he is sick. I just wanted to let you know the doctor said he shouldn't be moved till the fever drops, otherwise I would drive him home. If you could let his dad know he won't be in to work for a few days."

"I can come up, to help."

"No, it's fine. You don't need to; I am sure he will be fine. Umm, out of curiosity, has he had fevers before?"

"Yes, he has had a few."

"I don't know how to ask..."

"Why? What's going on, Emily?"

"Has he ever gotten violent before?"

"Violent? What has he done?"

"Look, it's probably nothing. Maybe he just caught me off guard," I said, trying to smooth it over. Last thing I needed was to have her think she needed to come out.

"No, he is not violent, even when ill. I will let his dad know not to expect him."

"Thank you."

"Not to change the topic, but did he ask you?"

"No, he never showed up on Friday. Was here late on Saturday, and it has been a pretty stressful weekend."

"Friday? But that was—"

"What?"

"No, it is not my place."

"Come on, Sylvia, it is your place. You are his mom."

"Well, I saw him Friday, he left work at noon. A woman picked him up from the job site."

"A woman?"

"Okay, it was her, but—"

"Sylvia, please don't make excuses. If he is seeing her again, that means he is cheating on me."

"Has he said anything to you about it?"

"No, he refused to tell me anything about why he was late and…" I stopped. Crap, I didn't want her to know.

"And…?"

"He's been sick. I don't want to read too much into what he has been saying," I said quickly. "The doctor said he could be delirious till the fever breaks."

"Okay. I will drop it for now, but we will talk more when I get out there," she said, and hung up the phone quickly before I could protest.

Great, more house guests. I was quickly running out of places to sleep. I guess I just had to hope that the fever would be gone by tomorrow, that James can get driven home by his mom, so Adam can stop thinking he needed to stay to protect me, so he can go home and then I could just worry about my sister and her upcoming wedding.

Chapter 4

I headed back up to James. He was groaning a bit when I walked in. I replaced the cold cloth on his head with a new one and stuck the other one in the ice water. I sat at the edge of the bed. I wanted to be furious at him, slap him and tell him to get out. He promised he wouldn't cheat on me again; it was the only reason I stayed with him. The first time, he said he was drinking at a business meeting, she offered to drive him home, and things happened. It had happened two other times with the same woman. This time, she picked him up from work. He could not use drinking as an excuse. And even though I didn't know the details, he was with her and showed up a day late. I couldn't be naïve and give him the benefit of the doubt any more. It was too late for that. Maybe if he would have explained from the beginning, told me the truth. But he tried to hide it, and then, was trying to accuse me…No, I had to stop thinking about it. His eyes, his intensity, scared the shit out of me, and I couldn't think about that right now. Right now, I had to care for him. I couldn't help but think about Adam in the next room, how much I wanted to go wake him up and…Again, not the right thoughts to be having. Besides, revenge sex might make me feel better, but wouldn't be fair to Adam.

The branches tapped the window from the raging storm outside. And each time it did, James would moan. It was stupid, I must have been imagining it. But it almost seemed like he was in pain, that the branches were hitting him instead of the window. Yup, I was going crazy.

I rung out a cold cloth and wiped some of the sweat off James's face. The cloth on his head was so hot, so I put a cold one on and left the room. Grabbing a glass of wine from the kitchen, I thought about my mom and dad. They were so much in love; that was all I wanted. I thought I had that with James, I thought I could have what they had. My dad was devastated when she died. It is what drove Raylene and I to move away, because he never got over losing her, and it was harder and harder to live with him because we could see in his eyes that the more we grew up, the more we looked like her, and that hurt him. I would come by in the summers to visit him and her grave. I would watch him spend so much time behind the cabin, talking to her gravestone. He had made one for her, so she could always be close. Mom's parents wouldn't let her body be buried here, they had her cremated and took the ashes, but Dad wanted the head stone. I think he even buried a box. My great grandpa and grandma were buried out there, and my grandma and grandpa. When my dad passed, I made sure he was buried next to my mom. Out here, there was no law saying we couldn't have our own private cemetery. I think quite a few families that lived out here did it. The ones that have lived out here for generations, like we have.

Going back upstairs, I was going to check on James, but something drew me toward Adam's room. I slowly opened the door. He looked so peaceful. Why did I never see him? I have known him forever, but I just realized how attractive he was. He had nicely toned abs, was tall, muscular. What woman wouldn't be attracted to a guy like him? Especially with his personality. Why was he still single?

I closed the door. Last thing I wanted was for him to wake up and see me watching him. I wouldn't want him to get the wrong idea. Not to mention that it would be really embarrassing and very inappropriate. I checked in on James, and went back to watching the fire, when the music box caught my eye. Sitting on the couch, I opened the lid. The music played; the ballerina danced. And behind it, the engraving that Adam added, *Forever waiting.*

"That is beautiful," Raylene said, coming up behind me. I slammed the lid shut.

"Holy crap," I yelled.

"I'm sorry, I didn't mean to scare you."

"Don't worry about it. I have been scared of my own shadow all weekend," I said with a slight smile.

"This weekend? So, you don't usually scare easy," she said, sitting down beside me.

"No, not this bad."

"That's weird."

"Yeah, but everything has been weird."

"So, what was it you didn't say this afternoon? You left stuff out."

"Supposedly, James was supposed to be proposing this weekend, and I just talked to his mom earlier and he was with a woman on Friday, which was probably why he showed up a day late."

"How did you know he was going to propose?"

"He asked his mom to go ring shopping with him and told her. She accidentally let it slip."

"Right. I highly doubt it was accidental. And the second part, do you really think he cheated on you?"

"He kinda has done it before, so unless he says otherwise, what am I supposed to think?"

"And you are still with him?"

"Yeah, he said it was a one-time thing, even though I found out later it was more like a three-time thing. But I had already forgiven him for the one I found out about and the others were before that, so it's not like I could go back on it, and I loved him. Or, at least at the time, I thought I did. It was around the time Dad died that I found out, and I needed him. I didn't have anyone else, so maybe I just thought…I don't know what I thought, or what to think now. This is so messed up. Oh, which reminds me, we are getting more company. James's mom insisted on coming up to care for James."

"Well, that is good."

"Good? How is it in any way, good?"

"Because it frees you up to do other things with me, or another man," she said, clearing her throat.

"I am still technically dating James. I can't break up with him in this condition. We need to talk, and at this point, he is not saying much. Not to mention I am not going after another man while my boyfriend's mom is around. Just a couple days ago, I was her soon-to-be daughter-in-law."

"Fine, I guess it wouldn't look good if you did that. But you can't tell me you haven't thought about it." I smiled.

"I am not saying a word," I said.

"Oh my, you have thought about it."

"Briefly, yes. But it wouldn't be fair to Adam."

"Why not, he gets sex out of the deal."

"Ray, oh my god, I can't believe you just said that."

"It's the truth. Right, Ben?"

"Not to lump all guys into one category, but yeah, pretty much true. No guy usually would turn down sex. Even if it was to get back at your boyfriend."

"How long have you been listening?" I asked, embarrassed.

"Just the sex part," he said innocently.

"I can't believe you two. You guys should get back to bed."

"Come on, Ben, I think she wants to be alone now that we put all these naughty ideas in her head," she said, smirking.

"That is not why," I said adamantly. "But you guys have a wedding to plan and being half asleep might not work too well."

"She's right, let's get back to bed," Ben said, and they left the room. I opened the music box again and let the melody play. I knew the song; I just couldn't place where I heard it before. I set it down on the table and closed my eyes. I started humming along with it. It sounded so familiar.

37

I awoke to knocking on the door. The sun was shining brightly when I opened my eyes. The music box was no longer on the table. I was covered up, laying on the couch. Adam answered the door half-dressed. It looked like he had just gotten out of the shower. *He looked...wow.* As quickly as that thought entered my head, it also left when I saw Sylvia come in.

"Sylvia, you must have been speeding to get here this early," I said, sitting up.

"My dear, it is not early, it is nearly noon." I couldn't believe I had slept in this late, or that no one woke me. "Where is my son?"

"I'll take you," I said, and took her to where James was sleeping.

"What is going on here, why is he tied up?" she said when we had gotten to his room.

"The doctor said it was for his safety," I replied.

"He doesn't need these," she said, and started removing them.

"It took both Ben and I to get him off Emily last night. The doctor wanted to make sure she felt safe, so he asked us to leave them on," Adam said, coming through the doorway.

"He couldn't, I don't believe..." When she looked at me, I didn't deny it. She was struggling, trying to believe her own son could do something like that. The same things that went through my mind the night before were probably going through hers. And seconds later, she didn't have to try. He had finished releasing his one hand that his mother had loosened, grabbed his mom by the shirt, and started yelling.

"We are going to die, all of us, he is going to kill us one by one. He wants her. He wants Emily." Adam rushed up to James and tried to pry his hand off Sylvia. He was easier to subdue from only having one hand free. Adam was able to get him tied up again. I pulled Sylvia out of the room.

"The doctor thinks the fever is the cause of his not making any sense." Sylvia couldn't speak. When she finally could, she simply couldn't believe her son could act that way.

"Why didn't you tell me?"

"I asked, sort of? I didn't know how to word it without worrying you."

"No, he has never acted like that," she said, still shocked. "Did the doctor say how long he would be...like this?"

"No, he was hoping the fever would start to go away today, but there is no guarantee. The doctor should be by later today. He can answer more than I can."

"Do you know who he was talking about? Who wants you? And what was all that about killing people?"

"I don't know, and no one around here is killing anyone. The doctor said he wouldn't make much sense." I could see she was getting frustrated at me not being able to give her the answers she wanted.

"And who is the half-naked man, are you cheating on my son? I know what he did was wrong, but there is no need to—"

"No, Adam is a friend. He works at the hardware store in town," I said, and proceeded to explain everything that had gone on with the windows, his truck, and then with James acting weird. I watched Adam come down the stairs during my explanation.

"Well, then, I guess I should be thanking him for protecting my daughter-in-law," she said, relieved. I could see a pained look spread over Adam's face.

"Well, let's not be hasty. He still has some explaining to do." She looked at me, baffled. "The woman." A look of rage started building.

"Look, my son—"

"Sylvia, please don't make excuses. You saw him with a woman, and he has done it before. I told him the last time, if it happened again, I was done."

"Maybe he had the fever then already, and she just took care of him."

"Maybe, but that is why I am saying we have to wait and see. Especially since he has not even asked yet," I said, mostly for Adam's sake. Though I wondered why I cared so much what he thought. I also couldn't help but wonder, if James was coherent, would he be talking about Adam, would it be Adam who wanted me, would James think Adam would kill people to have me? That was stupid. I was reading too much into what a delusional man was saying.

The doctor arrived later that evening. Sylvia spent most of her time with him, asking him questions and making sure everything that was possible was being done to help him. It was less than half the day that she was here, and she had tried to untie him three times. She kept forgetting or dismissing the idea that her son was violent.

The doctor assured her he was doing everything he could, and the best thing for him would be if she went home. He had several people looking after him. Of course, she refused. But I was still grateful to him for trying. Adam gave up the bedroom next to James's to let her stay in there, so she could be close to him. Raylene and Ben came home from a day of exploring, showing Ben her favorite spots as a kid where she liked to play.

"You," Sylvia said, seeing Raylene.

"What?" I asked. "This is my sister, Raylene, and her fiancé, Ben."

"No, it was her. She is the one that picked up James on Friday."

"She couldn't have, she wasn't even in town yet."

"Maybe, I just look like her?" Raylene said. Sylvia kept shaking her head, insisting Raylene was the woman. I finally managed to get Sylvia to go to bed. Raylene and Ben said they had to get an early start tomorrow, so they followed suit shortly after.

Adam helped me look after James through the night, in between a couple hours of sleep. By 5 a.m., Sylvia was up and said she would take over, so Adam and I could sleep.

Chapter 5

"Why does he want you so bad?" James asked, pinning me down on the couch by my shoulders. "What have you promised him? You weren't supposed to be his, you were supposed to be mine." His hands went from my shoulders to my neck.

I was choking, I couldn't breathe.

"Emily, wake up," Adam said, frantically shaking me awake. I sat up, coughing. "You okay?"

"Just a dream," I said, trying to catch my breath.

"I think it was more than a dream," Sylvia said from across the room.

"I agree," Adam said. "I don't know what it was about, but there are marks on your neck."

"What? That is ridiculous," I said, jumping to my feet. Sure enough, the place where James was strangling me in my sleep was starting to show signs of bruising. I pulled up the sleeves of the t-shirt and the shoulders were bruised as well.

"But that is impossible," I exclaimed. Adam saw all the bruising as well.

"What was the dream?" Adam asked. I didn't want to tell him. "It might be important if that is happening?" he said, pointing to my bruises.

"How?"

"I don't know, but with the way James is acting, and now this?"

"Adam, you were in the room while I was asleep."

"Yes...but I didn't." He looked hurt. "Sylvia was there too."

"No, Adam, not you. Could my dream have made me do this to myself?"

"Oh, no, your hands weren't there," he replied, seeming relieved that I was not accusing him.

"Adam, what is going on? Am I going crazy too?"

"No, I don't think so. I can't tell you why the bruising is happening, but maybe you should take some time for yourself. Maybe you are just worn out. I know your dad liked to talk to your mom to clear his head. Maybe it would help. Like you said, it has been weird and crazy for the last little while. Maybe talking it out might help." I nodded. I grabbed a quick bite to eat and some water and decided to go for a walk. I grabbed my camera just in case.

I started by walking to the lake. I remember him trying to teach me how to swim. Dad taking pictures from the dock. I walked along the dock. I noticed, with all the rain, the water was almost reaching the top of the dock. Any more rain and it would be under water. I looked over at the small cemetery. I hadn't been back there since we buried Dad two years ago. But maybe talking to his grave might help. It helped Dad, or maybe I just hoped it did. I mean, he was out there a lot. I shrugged and took a deep breath. What could it hurt to try? Slowly, I walked over and sat down. I looked at Dad's gravestone for a while. I didn't know what to say. Even if I did, where would I start?

I sighed and stood up.

"Emily," I heard a whisper right behind my ear. I screamed, turned around. No one was there. Adam came running around the corner.

"You okay?"

"That wasn't you, was it? I swear, if you are trying to scare me, this isn't a good time."

"I was out front. They are here with the tow truck to get my wreck out of here. What's going on?"

"I am obviously going crazy," I said, throwing my hands up, as if surrendering and accepting that I was going completely nuts.

"You just need to relax. And even if it sounds crazy, talk to them." He nodded toward my parents' graves. "You will feel better." He took my hand and gave it a squeeze, and went back to the front of the house.

"Sure, why not," I said, sitting back down. I didn't believe it could help, but what the hell. So, I started rambling and rambling. I didn't even realize when it had gotten dark out. I stood up to go inside, but something caught my eye...I looked back to the headstones and saw a ghostly figure, my dad? The image of him was not clear, more like a silhouette of someone you would see in a fog. But it had to be him, right? I could almost touch him, but each time I moved forward, it was if I was standing still and he was the same distance away.

"Don't be afraid," he said softly. "I have been waiting, a really long time, for you."

"Dad, it has only been two years. What are you talking about?"

"You need to know."

"What? What do I need to know?"

"Emily, I need to tell you," he said, reaching out toward me, and then he was gone.

"Emily." I heard my name being called again. I opened my eyes. I was laying on the ground between my parent's graves. Great, more hallucinating. Just what I needed.

"Emily." I heard again. It sounded farther away. Not the voice from before.

"Coming." It was James calling me. I ran in the house hoping he was better, hoping he was no longer…I was puzzled how I could hear him clearly when he wasn't yelling. It sounded as if he was in the next room.

"Emily," he said again. It was louder, as I reached the top of the stairs. I opened the door to his room.

"Emily," he said again. His eyes were closed, and his lips didn't move, but I heard him.

"I'm here," I said, and sat on the bed next to him. Maybe I just imagined that he was calling me.

"I'm cold," he said, opening his eyes. "Why am I—" he stopped when he tried to move his hands and couldn't. "Why…tied."

"One sec, I'll be right back. Okay?" I said hurriedly. He nodded, still trying to move. I ran out of the room and found Adam first, and asked him to call the doctor. Found Sylvia, asked her to get some water, then ran to get James some extra blankets. When I got back to the room, Sylvia was already in there trying to get him to drink some water. She looked so happy.

"Can we take—" Sylvia started to say.

"Soon, we will wait for the doctor, just to make sure," I said. She nodded through her tears. She was overjoyed that he was actually making sense.

"Hungry," he managed to get out, after drinking some more. Sylvia jumped up and went to go make him some soup. "Why am I tied?"

"You weren't yourself," I told him.

"What…what does that mean?" he struggled out.

"She means you attacked her," Adam said, coming in the room, eyeing James coldly. He leaned back against the wall and crossed his arms in front of him, watching.

"Why?" I could see he was having trouble speaking.

"We don't know. The doctor says it was 'cause of your fever," I said. I needed him to stop asking about it. This was awkward enough.

"How long?"

"I guess that depends on the last thing you remember, but at least a couple of days. I am going to check on how the soup is coming along. You should rest. The doctor should be here soon," I said, looking at Adam.

"Yeah, he is on his way," he said, speaking up, still staring at James.

"Okay, so you rest, and we can talk a bit later." He nodded. His mom passed us on the way down the stairs, so I turned around and followed her back to James's room. She was in her own little world, waiting on her son hand-and-foot; I watched from the doorway. Anything that happened while he was sick was forgotten in her mind. He was her baby boy, and he needed her.

Less than five minutes later, the doctor showed up. He cleared him for removing the restraints, but told him he was still not allowed to get out of bed. He said he would be back in two days to check on him again. I breathed a sigh of relief that he was back to normal. Soon, he and his mom could leave. This was not the time to discuss the other woman with him. As much as I wanted to, I couldn't. I needed to talk to him badly, tell him of my doubts, needed him to reassure me.

"How is he?" Raylene asked, when she and Ben got home that night.

"Good. Doctor says Sylvia might be able to take him home in a couple days."

"Good," she said quickly. Ben watched her as she went upstairs.

"I bet you are happy that he will be okay," Ben said.

"Yes, it is really good news."

"If all goes well, everything should slow down in a couple days hopefully. Raylene, I know, has been trying to keep busy, 'cause she didn't want to bother you. But I think she would really like to spend some time with you."

"Yeah, slowing things down might be nice. And spending more time with Ray would be really nice too."

"I guess I should head to bed as well, have a good night."

"Goodnight."

A little while later Ben walked down the stairs again.

"Why are you with him?" Ben yelled at me. "He doesn't love you. I love you. I have loved you from the moment we met; I have taken care of you. You need to get rid of him or I will." I slapped Ben across the face.

"What?" he said, looking shocked.

"You were sleepwalking," I said. "You should get back to bed."

"Yeah, okay," he said, and left, shaking his head.

"You know what he was talking about?"

"No, I don't think he did either," I said, turning to Adam who was laying on the floor in front of the fireplace.

"If I ever start acting weird, you will let me know, won't you?"

"Of course I would."

"I bet you will be glad when things get back to normal."

"Honestly, it has only been a week, but even as crazy as it has been, this is starting to feel normal," I said. He laughed.

"Oh, some stuff arrived for you today by courier. I stacked it by the door."

"Thank you, Adam." I propped myself up on my elbow. "I mean it, thank you for staying with me through all this."

"No problem. Wouldn't miss all this for the world. We can't get entertainment like this in this town very often," he said, laughing.

"I'm serious."

"Okay, I'm sorry."

"Could I ask you a question?"

"Sure."

"Will you give me an honest answer?"

"Okay," he said, sitting up.

"The engraving in the music box, why did you write it?"

"It was something…Look, I really shouldn't have put it in there. You are with James, and it was a while ago. I heard your dad say it at your mom's grave all the time and—"

"You were there when he talked to her?"

"Sometimes."

"What would he tell her?"

"Everything. He talked about what would happen that day. How quickly you guys were growing up. He talked a lot about how he thought he was losing Raylene. He never knew what to do with her."

"I can't believe he would let you sit with him."

"It was only a few times. I think he needed it, just to make sure someone was listening." I nodded. "He must have felt so alone after she died."

"Aren't you going to ask?"

"What?"

"If he said anything about you?"

"No, if he was sitting at Mom's grave, it was a conversation between them. Just 'cause he let you listen doesn't mean I should know what was said." He shrugged and laid back down, so did I. Only, I lied. I did want to know, really badly, but I didn't want to ask.

"He thought you were strong, he thought you could handle anything." I smiled. I didn't believe that, but I am glad he said it. Maybe one day I would ask him for the truth. But for tonight, I went to sleep thinking that he truly did say it.

The next day, as Adam changed the bandages on my hand and arm, Sylvia came running down the stairs, out of breath.

"Emily, come and talk to him. He is trying to get out of bed to see you. He is getting really bored up there." I told her I would be up soon. The cut on my leg didn't need re-bandaging. It was healing quicker than the other two.

"So, I hear you are bored up here," I said, walking into James's room.

"Yes, not that I don't appreciate you being here, Mom, but could I talk to Emily alone?"

"Sure," she said, and left the room.

"So, Mom has been very vague about what happened. Maybe you could fill me in?"

"What do you remember?"

"I remember driving out here. Falling on my face, you coming out, showering, going to bed, and nothing much else after that."

"You were not yourself. You had a fever."

"I guess I did something bad."

"It wasn't that bad; you just got a bit rough."

"With Adam? He could have just left."

"No, with me. Adam and Ben had to pull you off me. And Adam wasn't comfortable leaving with you being the way you were." Then, he saw my neck.

"Oh, god, did I do that?" I didn't know what to say. *Yeah, I had a dream of you strangling me and woke up with it.*

"No, I don't know how I got this." Great, that sounded worse out loud.

"Did Adam do that?" he asked, getting upset.

"No, Adam hasn't hurt me."

"Not like I did," he said. "That is what you mean, isn't it?"

"No, it is not what I meant, James. I just didn't want you to think that he did."

"So, I did it, and you just don't want to tell me so I don't feel bad."

"James, don't worry about this, it wasn't you." Since I couldn't explain, I didn't want to continue this conversation. "You need to worry about getting better."

"I'm fine." I sat down on the bed beside him.

"Then I need to ask you something. And I don't want you to go into details, but were you with a woman on Friday, before you came out here? And did you sleep with her?"

"I have to exp—"

"No, James. I just need a yes or no. I will believe you."

"Yes, to both," he said, and closed his eyes not to look at me. Tears started welling in my eyes. I guess I had known already, and even though it hurt to hear it, I am glad I knew.

"Okay," I said, gulping back sobs.

"Emily, I'm—"

"Please, don't. I don't need to know you are sorry. I don't need to hear that you swear you will never do it again. I can't."

"Emily, I need—"

"No, James. I don't need an explanation. I don't need you to get it off your chest just so you can have a clear conscience. So, you and your mom can stay till the doctor says you are better and can travel. After that, I need you to go. I wish you the best, James, but we are done." Now it was him that let the tears fall from his eyes.

"Okay."

"I will send your mom back in," I said and got up to leave. He grabbed my hand.

"I am sorry," he said, and let me go. I left the room, not looking back.

"Sylvia, you can go back in now." I decided to go through the packages delivered by the courier, to try and get my mind off of the realization of what I had just done. Maybe he did have a really good explanation, was I being too hard on him by not hearing him out? No, he knew exactly what he was doing and what I would do if he did it. I opened the boxes. Some were photos I had taken that I had sent out to get framed by an acquaintance of mine in the city that does the custom framing.

"Hey, wanna drive into town and get the windows ordered?" Adam said, coming in from outside. I shook my head.

"The keys are in the bowl by the door, if you wanted to take my car," I said, and turned away from him, so he wouldn't see the look on my face. He grabbed them and left. Raylene and Ben did the same. After dinner, I asked Raylene to take a walk with me.

"So, I am assuming this walk was to talk?" I nodded and told her about James and my conversation. She stayed quiet till I was done. "Do you know who?"

"No, I told him not to tell me. I didn't want to know details."

"I guess it might be good to leave it at that."

"Yeah, not much more to say." We got back to the house late; everyone was already asleep.

I laid on the couch. Maybe I was overreacting. What if he did have a good reason for…No, I told him last time, if he did it again, it would be over. No sense in going through all the trust issues again. But could I throw out four years? I mean, he helped me through Dad's death, and…Stop. I just needed to stop making excuses for him.

The doctor said James was well enough to travel, but should probably not drive.

Ben and Adam helped James into his mom's car. And they left shortly after.

It felt weird after four years together that I was feeling nothing. I felt hurt that he would cheat on me, but not that we were no longer together. It was almost a relief? Maybe that wasn't the right word, but after all this time, knowing that I didn't have to worry about him going behind my back or wondering if he was lying to me about why he was late from work. I couldn't go through all that again. I worked for most of the day, taking walk around the lake, taking photographs. It helped to get my mind off James. I felt a bit guilty. Shouldn't I have felt more? I was in love with him, was ready to say yes to him; I was ready to get married to him. And I am already thinking of him in past tense. I sat down on a bench at one of the parks around the lake. Did I fool myself into thinking I cared for him more than I actually did? Did I actually care for him? My head was swimming; I didn't know what to think anymore. Was I even a good girlfriend, is that why he felt he needed to cheat on me? I sat at that bench till it started getting dark. I snapped another roll of pictures when the sun was setting.

By the time I got back to the cabin, Raylene had already cleaned up Sylvia's room as well as mine. Adam did the grocery shopping and by dinner time, I was hoping I would be feeling better, and that things would get back to normal. I almost was going to ask Adam why he was still hanging around since James was gone, I didn't need protecting anymore. But I didn't. I didn't need another argument right now; I didn't need another person to walk out of my life right now either. It was comforting to have him here, and maybe in some way, he knew that.

After Raylene and Ben went to bed in the room Sylvia had been in, I went to clean up the other guest bedroom that had not been cleaned yet. I needed to keep myself busy; I had to stop thinking about James. Later that night, Adam handed me a glass of wine and we sat in front of the fireplace.

"How are you holding up?"

"I am actually doing okay."

"Do you regret breaking it off?"

"How did you…?"

"Raylene told me." I nodded. I guess I should have expected it.

"No."

"You probably don't want to talk about this, do you?"

"Nope, not really," I said, sipping my wine.

"What do you want to talk about?"

"Do we have to talk?"

"No, I guess—" he started. I didn't let him finish. I covered his mouth with mine, but he pushed me back.

"Not that I am saying no, but are you sure?"

"Yes," I said, unbuttoning his shirt slowly. I kissed him again softly. He hesitated at first, but that didn't last. He set the glasses of wine down and pulled me close; his kiss started slow and grew more heated. I wanted him. Grabbing his hand, I led him up to my bedroom.

Chapter 6

A couple days later, I was in the kitchen drinking coffee when Raylene and Ben came downstairs and left the house, giggling, which was also the time James and his dad showed up. I let them in for coffee.

"We just came to pick up his car," he said.

"Sure."

"Look, my son told me what he did."

"I don't want to talk about it."

"I think it deserves a conversation after all the time you two were together."

"I appreciate what you are trying to do, but no, it does not. There is no need to discuss anything."

"You should at least listen to what he has to say."

"Why?"

He didn't know what to say.

"Dad, it's fine, she is right. I don't deserve her sympathy. She only followed through with—" Just then Adam came down in boxers. "So, this is why you don't care, 'cause you had another guy waiting," he said, getting mad.

"No, and you know what, James, you have no right to get mad. Take it like a fucking man. You screwed up, not me. At least I waited till I told you we were done. Now get out," I said, stepping in between the two men. The look in their eyes said it all, they were getting ready to do the macho crap.

"James, let's go, it's done." Now I understood why James brought his dad. He wanted him to convince me to take him back. After seeing Adam, he realized I wouldn't. They left. James burned rubber, trying to get out of the driveway. I closed the door.

"Thank you for not saying anything. I am sure he would have done more if—"

"If I would have rubbed it in his face that I got you," he said, laughing.

"Yeah."

"It's not a competition. I had no reason to do any of that. Besides, as far as I knew, you were just doing a rebound thing. Why would I rub that in?"

"Adam, it wasn't a rebound thing. But I also don't know where it will go."

"And I am okay with that. If what you need right now is no attachments and just sex, I am more than happy to help. 'Cause if I am being honest, sex with you is great," he said, kissing me on the cheek. "Breakfast?" he said, grinning at me.

"Sure." I could see he didn't want to discuss it anymore. But something was off in the way he spoke, almost as if he didn't believe what he was saying. Was he actually okay with it? Maybe he only said it because I was unsure, and didn't want to push me.

That night at dinner, it was really quiet. I asked Raylene to come for a walk with me.

"So how are things with you, Ray? Happy to be engaged? Having fun with wedding planning?"

"Things are good, yes, and yes. I thought it would feel different, but honestly, it doesn't. Maybe I will feel more when we are actually married."

"Maybe."

"I am sorry it didn't work out with James."

"Things happen for a reason. I can't say I understand why, but who am I to argue with fate? I should have known the first time he cheated. I chose to ignore it."

"You believe in fate?"

"How can I not? With all the signs?"

"Does that mean you will listen to fate about Adam?"

"What do you mean?"

"Come on, he has been with you through all of this, expecting nothing in return. He has been hanging around since we were kids. Has never married."

"So?"

"Come on, he has been in love with you since before I took off. How could you not see it?"

"That is ridiculous. He does not love me. He would have said something, or at least hinted at it."

"Really? Are you sure about that? Maybe he was waiting for you to notice him."

"Ray, stop matchmaking, I just got out of a relationship. If something happens with Adam and me, it will happen. If not, then it won't." She was smiling.

"Hasn't something already happened? The walls of the cabin are not sound proof." I covered my face with my hands. "Hey, I'm not judging. I think it was me who told you to jump him days ago."

"Oh my god, Ray, stop. From now on, Adam topics are off limits to you."

A few days later, I was in town, mailing off some of my rolls of film. People always thought I was weird for not switching to digital, but there is something to be said for old-school photos; I couldn't help it. I stopped in to see Adam at work, taking him a coffee.

"Rain is moving in. There is going to be a lot of it. The plastic should hold, but just in case, might want to think keeping some boards handy." I nodded. He also gave me an update that the windows wouldn't arrive till next week, so he would bring them out the weekend after that. Raylene was obviously wrong about the way Adam felt. He was acting normal, like he always was. I, however, was not, and I really hoped that he wouldn't notice. But I didn't want to seem too eager to get him into bed again. I mean, we had those couple of days. Great, just thinking about it was making my cheeks hot. Oh, crap, was I blushing, could he see it? Looking at him, if he did see, he did not show it.

I stopped at the post office on the way home. After making myself a cup of coffee, I sat on the porch. Most were bills, one was an envelope with no return address. If I would have known who it was from, I would have never opened it.

Dear Emily,

I know you have every right to hate me, and I don't blame you. But I need you to give me a chance to explain, rather than waiting for you to say yes or no to seeing me. I am going to come out the cabin. Maybe things will work out better than the last two times.

I won't tell you when I am coming, just so you won't purposely not be there, but I will give you some time to calm down or collect your thoughts or whatever you need to do.

I am not going to ask you to forgive me, at least, not right away. I just need to see you. To talk to you.

Please.

The letter ended with that. Just please. Currently, I didn't know what I would do when I saw him. Maybe him giving me time was not a bad idea on his part, although his showing up whenever he wanted to wasn't a good idea.

The rain started pouring down. I went back inside, made a snack, and sat in front of the fireplace. I liked watching the fire, listening to the crackle and pop.

"Dad, I don't understand what is going on. You said you had something to tell me?"

"Yes, I should have told you long ago. I need you to understand it is not my fault. I don't know when it all started going so wrong. So terribly wrong."

"Dad, what did? How can you be here?"

"I am not really here, you just needed someone to talk to and your mind came up with me."

"So, I am talking to myself. Great, that is a sure sign of insanity." He smiled.

"Emily, have you added it yet?"

"Not intentionally. It got brought in the cabin, but I am not engaged. So, it shouldn't count. Raylene and Ben did. But why do I need to explain all this to you? Aren't you me? Shouldn't you already know everything I know?"

"I do, but this is your mind's way of sorting through the information. You did this with your mom when she died. But you were still young, you may not remember." A look of pain came over his face.

"Dad, what's wrong?"

"If your item is added, then I am sorry, but it is too late, for both of you—"

"Emily, what are you doing out here, it's pouring," Raylene said, coming up to me. "Come on, let's go inside." I was confused. How had I even gotten outside? I was looking at the fire the last time...Raylene got me back inside and we both dried off.

"Are you okay? Why were you out there?"

"Dad. I wanted to talk to him. He wanted to warn me about something."

"Emily?" Raylene said, worried.

"He said it was too late."

"For what?"

"I don't know, he didn't say."

"Emily, have you seen him before? Does he talk to you a lot?"

"Just once. Adam thought with all that was happening, I should do what he did. He would go out and talk to Mom all the time. So, I went to talk to him. He sounded so scared for us, Ray."

"Emily, you know that is not normal, right?"

"Ray, it wasn't actually him. It was my mental projection of him, just someone to talk to." I don't think I convinced her that I wasn't crazy.

"Let's get you into bed." I wasn't tired, but I didn't argue.

"She is acting strange," I heard her whisper through the door.

"Do you think we should call the doctor?"

"Maybe give it a day or so, see if she gets better?"

"Okay."

"She said she saw Dad. More than once."

"How 'bout we call Adam? He can keep an eye on her more than we can. If we do it, it might seem suspicious. If he does it, he is just spending time with her."

"Okay." I rolled over and looked at the wall. My eyes started playing tricks on me. They saw the walls moving like a heartbeat. I closed my eyes. When I opened them again, they were back to normal.

Maybe I was sick, like James. I closed my eyes again. I just needed sleep. I haven't slept well for a while.

I opened my eyes and saw a shadow in the corner. I opened my mouth to scream, but a hand clamped over my mouth. It was Adam.

"Sorry, I didn't mean to scare you, your sister was worried. Said you were seeing your dad." I nodded.

"I told her it wasn't real; it was like you said I needed to talk to someone. My mind created him, so I wouldn't feel like I was talking to myself. But, Adam, he said it was too late, for both Ray and me."

"I'm sorry. I thought encouraging you to talk to him would be a good thing."

"It's okay. I just won't do it again."

"Did he say what you were too late for?"

"No." Adam sounded relieved in a way, which was weird, but for right now, I was more relieved that he was here. He laid down next to me. I listened to the rhythmic thumping of his heart beating next to my ear and fell asleep.

I woke up later, Adam was not there. A crack of lightning by my window made me scream.

"What's wrong?" Adam said, rushing into the room.

"Nothing." I gasped, grabbing my chest. "The lightning was so close to the house."

"Oh yeah, it started about an hour ago," he said, and came to lay back down beside me.

"Thank you for being here, Adam. I can't even imagine what you must be thinking about our family."

"I'm just glad I could help. When you guys moved away, it was like a void in town. Everyone noticed." Another streak of lightning flashed in front of the window; it was deafening.

"I wish I knew what was wrong with me."

"Do you think there is something wrong?"

"Yes, maybe, I don't know. I have been seeing things, hearing voices call my name. I have been scared of everything. This has never happened before."

"I am always going to be here if you need to talk or whatever," he said casually. I smiled at the 'whatever' part.

"Emily," I heard a whisper from outside the door.

"Do you hear it?" I asked, looking at Adam.

"Hear what?"

"Someone calling me." He shrugged and stood next to me, grabbing my hand and opening the door. There was no one there.

"Emily," I heard again, but this time, it was coming from downstairs. Pulling Adam along with me, I made my way down the stairs.

I heard my name called one more time from the dining-room area. There was no one there.

"Okay?" he asked.

"Yeah, just hearing things I guess."

"Okay, then back to bed it is." I nodded, and he pulled me along back up the stairs.

I woke up. There was no sign of storms, the birds were chirping, and except for a strong wind, only signs of storm were the mud puddles along the sides of the road. Today, the windows were arriving. No more looking at the plastic.

Adam and his dad refused to let me and Raylene help with the windows. Ben was allowed to help with some of it. Raylene and I sat on the porch, drinking coffee, laughing at the conversation above us. Ben had caught his sleeve in between the window frame and the wall, they were trying to pull it out without removing the whole window.

Glancing down the road, I stiffened, as I saw James's car driving up. He said he would come to talk to explain. Before he even got to the house, the hairs on the back of my neck were standing on end. Raylene looked at me and was about to leave.

"Don't go."

"But this has nothing to do with me."

"Please don't, just in case he is not himself." I saw hesitation in her eyes, but she stayed.

James walked up to the porch and looked at the two of us.

"Can we talk?" he asked.

"You can talk, but Ray is staying here," I stated.

"So, I guess you know then?"

"Know that you were cheating on me, yes. You told me that before you left, it is why I dumped you." He looked at Raylene and then back to me.

"I didn't know who she was. I am sorry."

"It doesn't matter who she was, the fact is you did it, after promising you wouldn't."

"Look, I don't know what she told you, but she found me."

"Your mom didn't tell me anything."

"What? No, not my mom. Raylene."

"Ray? What does she have to do with you cheating?"

"Because it was her."

"What? You are not making any sense."

"The girl I was cheating on you with was your sister. But I didn't know she was your sister."

"No, that is a lie. My sister was not even in town then. She is with Ben."

"I should go," Raylene said.

"No, tell her," James said. I looked at Raylene who couldn't meet my eyes.

"This is between the two of you," she said, trying to stay out of the conversation.

"Ray, just tell him he is mistaken. You weren't in town then." She didn't say anything.

"Just tell her, damn it," he said, punching the post of the railing. It happened so fast.

I screamed. Raylene screamed. James collapsed to his knees, and then slumped over. Sticking out of the top of his head was a piece of glass.

Our screams had the guys rushing to us. Blood was pouring out of the top of James's head. Through our sobs, we tried to explain what happened. Both Ben and Adam were trying to calm a hysterical Raylene and I down, while Adam's dad called the doctor and checked to see if he was alive.

He shook his head.

"Have to get the rest of the glass off the roof. We can't have this happening to anyone else. Oh, dear god, what is Sylvia going to say?" It made me sick just thinking about it. I knew I had to call her. But, how could I? No, I couldn't do it. I started shaking uncontrollably. Ben went to get the glass off the roof after he got Raylene to calm down. Adam got me and Raylene a blanket.

A short time later, we had the doctor, the police, and the coroner at the cabin.

One by one, they took our statements. I gave them Sylvia's number to call her. I couldn't believe it. One second, he was standing there, the next he was lying on the steps, with blood pooling around his head, the jagged piece of glass sticking out of the top.

I was glad when it was all over and they had his body moved. It did not remove the pictures of his lifeless body from my mind. I had been with him for so long and having him lying there was painful to see.

"You should get some rest," Raylene said.

"I can't leave it there," I replied, and grabbed cleaning supplies from the kitchen. I had to get rid of the blood. As I cleaned, I cried. Yes, he cheated on me, and it was like a knife to the chest, but he didn't deserve this.

He cheated. He said it was with Raylene. His mom recognized her. But she couldn't have been. She wasn't in town. Was she? Could she have come in a few days before she showed up?

No, not tonight. I couldn't handle anymore. Tonight was for James. I thought about the good times. The day he made me play hooky from work to take me to the Star Trek movie marathon at the theater. They were playing all six original movies. He knew how much of a sci-fi nerd I was.

I remembered the day we ran into his mom shopping. It was a couple days after she walked in on us having sex. He was so embarrassed that he tried to hide before she could see him. But she saw him anyway. It was an awkward day for both of them. Or, there was the time he rented a sea doo and stalled it in the middle of the lake. It took two hours for someone to find us and tow us back to shore. We spent the rest of the weekend putting aloe on each other. We were so burnt.

Then there was the freezing November day he dared me to go skinny dipping, saying he would do it if I did. I jumped in and he ended up chickening out but was very helpful in warming me up afterward. My tears dropped down onto his pool of blood. I sat down and hugged my knees. I appreciated that no one came out to help me, although I could feel their eyes on me every now and then.

"What did you do? You killed him. He loved you and you killed him," Sylvia said, running up to me and slapping me across the face. James's dad came up behind her to restrain her. Had I really been out here for that long? Sylvia standing in front of me must mean that I had been.

"She loved him too, dear."

"No, she didn't, she left him." She calmed down enough for him to let her go and came after me again. Just when she was going to slap me again, Adam grabbed her hand.

"This is not Emily's fault."

"Let my wife go," James's dad said sternly. Adam released his grip.

"You, you took her away from my son," Sylvia said, glaring at Adam.

"No, Sylvia, your son cheated on me. I wanted to marry him, and he cheated on me."

"With your sister," she said, looking at Raylene, who was standing in the doorway. "You sent your sister after my son, so you would have a reason to leave him."

"My sister has been travelling for the last 12 years. I haven't heard from her much. I told you that already. And why would I want James to cheat on me? That is twisted that you would think I would do something like that."

"Enough," Ben said, standing firmly beside Raylene. "Why are you here?"

"I needed directions to get to the doctor's house," James's dad said quickly, knowing this could escalate quickly. Adam knew the area and helped him with directions so they could leave.

We thought we were in the clear with Sylvia, but then she saw the dark spot on the porch that I was still working on in between me crying and thoughts of James, and that sent her back into rage and hysteria. Ben helped James's dad put her back in the car. I returned to cleaning up the blood.

"No matter how much you scrub, his blood will always be on your hands," she screamed out the window.

"Don't listen to her," Adam said. "She is just upset. It was not your fault."

"Yes, it is. I left the glass on the roof."

"You got hurt, and then James got sick. Honestly, I had forgotten all about it."

"That is not an excuse. She was right. Look, I know you are trying to help, but could I please be alone?" He looked hurt but went in the house. I caught a glimpse of him watching me through the window. I guess I couldn't blame him for keeping an eye on me. He has done nothing but try to help since this whole situation started. I felt bad.

I finished cleaning up the blood and went back inside. I looked around, but everyone had made themselves scarce. I cleaned myself up, then went to look for Adam. He wasn't in my room. Maybe he thought I needed more space. I went to the spare bedroom. He was asleep. I carefully climbed into bed beside him and pulled his arm around me. He squeezed my hand lightly. Okay, so he wasn't asleep, he just didn't want to be pushy.

"I'm sorry," I whispered. "I shouldn't have snapped at you." I felt him kiss the back of my neck.

"You went through a lot tonight. You can behave anyway you want, or feel any way you need to," he whispered back.

"I don't think it was my fault. You were right about that."

"Good. I like to be right." I could hear the smile in his voice even though I wasn't looking at him. "You are still not sure, are you?"

"About?"

"Raylene. You have your doubts?"

"How can they both say it was her? Why would they lie?"

"I can't answer that."

"I know. What sucks is that now if I say nothing, it is going to drive me crazy. But do I really want to know the truth? I don't want to ruin the relationship; I just got her back." He didn't say anything, he just held me tightly.

I couldn't sleep. Every time I closed my eyes, I would see James dying over and over again. I would see him lying in the blood. Each time, I would jolt myself awake, and each time, Adam would give me a gentle squeeze, reassuring me he was watching over me. When the light started peering through the window, I forced myself out of bed. There was no point struggling anymore.

Adam said he had to leave for a bit to get a change of clothes, and do a few errands, but that he would be back later. I gave him a long hug; I didn't want to let him go. He promised he would be back as soon as he could. I sat on the porch, trying to forget the dreams. Trying to forget that I was sitting not more than five feet from where James died.

James was dead. Why would that thought not seem real? I watched it happen yesterday. Why did it feel so far away? I didn't know how to feel. He was the first person that I watched die right in front of me. It is different from getting the phone call, with those, you can't do nothing about it; the person is already dead, like with my dad or my mom. But to see it happen in front of you in seconds and not be able to stop it. To watch it unfold in front of you and…I kept going over it in my mind. I didn't want to. I needed a distraction. Is that cold of me? Was it wrong of me to try and move on so quickly? He hurt me multiple times, is that how I was justifying wanting to forget?

"You shouldn't feel bad. There was nothing you could have done," Dad said, sitting with his back to the gravestone.

"Dad?"

"It's nice of you to come visit."

"Did I? How did I?"

"Just accept it. Don't you like talking to me? Seeing me?"

"Yes, but you are not real."

"Of course I'm not, but that doesn't mean we can't talk. You obviously have something on your mind."

"But I can't, I'm not crazy."

"No one said you are, Sweety, but this might be your way of dealing with whatever situation you might be in." I gave up arguing with him. I told him the situation, with James, and the possible situation with Raylene. The stuff with Adam.

"Emily, are you all right?" I woke up to Raylene shaking me awake.

"I'm fine," I said, looking around. Somehow, I ended up at the graveyard. I didn't remember coming out here. Not wanting Raylene to worry, I didn't say anything.

"I made lunch; you should come get some."

"I'll be in, in a minute." She left. I turned back to the grave and ran my fingers over his name. "Thanks, Dad, kind of sneaky, but very appreciated." He helped me sleep. I slept and did not see James. I slept for the whole morning and felt happier. Even though it was a dream, I felt much better just being able to talk to him. Maybe Adam was right. I would have to tell him that, I thought, smiling. I went inside to join Raylene.

I tried to act normal around Raylene, but the nagging of James's words kept entering my head.

"Ray, please be honest. Was it you…with James?"

"How can you ask that?"

"Because two people said it was you, and honestly, it was just me assuming you were not in town. For all I know, you could have been here."

"Why would I do something like that to you?"

"You might not have known he was with me. I don't know."

"I don't know what to say, Emily, I—"

"Never mind, I am being stupid, you wouldn't cheat on Ben."

There was a knock on the door. It was James's parents.

"We spent all night with the doctor and the cops, and they said there was no foul play. It was just a wrong place at the wrong time thing. My wife wanted to sue, but I have since talked her out of it. I know you loved my son, and that you must be having a hard time with this as well."

"Thank you. I am really sorry for your loss." He nodded.

"Well, I just wanted to let you know; I am sorry my son hurt you. I also wanted to ask you not to come to the funeral, my wife just calmed down. I don't think it would be wise for you to attend," he said, and turned to leave.

"I understand. Thank you for coming by." He nodded again and hurried away.

"That was nice of him," Raylene said, coming around the corner.

"Yes, it was." Ben drove up and asked Raylene to go into town to get groceries with him. Excitedly, she agreed. Sitting still, apparently, was not something she liked to do. She also was never the type to dwell on things, she moved on quickly ever since she was a kid. There are times I wished I could be more like her.

I realized, after they drove off, that Raylene never answered my question, although I kind of realized that I gave her the out by thinking she wouldn't cheat on Ben. I decided to clean. Hopefully to get my mind off things.

Chapter 7

Adam showed up by dinner time. As we lay in bed after further distractions, he mentioned that his parents invited us to dinner.

"Adam, I don't know, it's just kind of too soon—"

"I already told them it is not serious between us. They just thought if you needed to get out or talk about stuff. I mean, they knew your family and thought—"

"Actually, that does sound nice. With this whole Ray and James thing, a night talking about something else might be nice," I said, after thinking about it for a while.

"I was wondering, did you talk to her about it?"

"I asked, she dodged the question. She asked how I could ask something like that."

"Oh, that is not a good sign."

"Tell me about it. I wanted to give her the benefit of the doubt, but… What am I supposed to think now?"

"Give it time, ask her again…Maybe after she has a couple drinks," he said, laughing.

"As bad as that sounds, it might be what I have to do."

"Anything else on your mind?"

"Well, I know you like to hear you were right. So, you were right. I talked to my dad again today. I told him everything that was going on and I felt so much better." He leaned over and kissed the top of my head.

"You can tell me I am right anytime. What did he say?"

"He didn't get a chance. Ray woke me up before he could say anything. The weird part was, I was on the porch, but when Ray woke me up, I was at his grave."

"You have started sleepwalking, what is so strange about that?"

"I never did it before."

"You also were probably not under this much stress before."

"May—" I stopped.

"Emily," I heard a whisper from outside the door.

61

"What?" Adam asked.

"Someone is calling me." Adam got up and answered the door. There was no one there. I was relieved because he opened the door naked.

"Emily," I heard again. It was louder. I wrapped a sheet around me and descended the stairs. The voice was coming from the dining room. Adam stayed behind me, but kept silent.

"Emily, check the drawer," the voice whispered right behind my ear, which made me scream and run to Adam for cover. I saw the spirit hand pointing at the china cabinet.

"I don't know what you are hearing, but if it is voice, I don't think it can hurt you."

"Yeah, well, you let me know, if someone who isn't there whispers something in your ear, wouldn't freak you out?"

"Point taken."

"Why are you okay with this?"

"What do you mean?"

"Me hearing voices. You don't think I am insane? If you told me you were hearing voices, I would be calling the doctor right away."

"When the voices start telling you to kill people, maybe. Right now, it wants you in the dining room."

"Adam, I didn't know you were so okay with the supernatural."

"I can't say it isn't real, there are too many proven instances. Why couldn't it happen?"

"It has never happened to me before, why should it start now?"

"Maybe the spirits have never needed to talk to you before. Or they couldn't. I am just guessing, of course."

"You seem to have a lot more knowledge on this than you are telling me."

"There are local legends that get passed down in the families here. I guess, since you moved away, your dad never got the chance to tell you."

"So, spill."

"No, when you come for dinner at my parents, I will get them to tell you. In the meantime, let's not piss off the spirit. If he told you to do something, you should do it."

"First of all, the he is a she, and secondly, I don't know what she wants me to do," I said, looking around.

"What did she say?"

"She said to look in the drawer. But I don't know what it wants me to look for, there are only photographs in the drawers."

"Well, I guess you are taking a trip down memory lane. Come on, I will make some coffee."

"So how is it that this is not freaking you out?" I asked, seating myself in the kitchen with the first stack of photographs.

"Probably because I am not seeing or hearing what you are," he shrugged and said casually.

"So, you are not concerned that I am crazy?"

"Do you think you are?"

"Honestly, maybe a bit."

"Really?" he said, raising an eyebrow.

"Well, ever since James, I, yeah. I have been getting worried." He moved over to me and started rubbing my shoulders.

"I for one don't think you are going crazy."

"Oh yeah, and what makes you so sure?"

"Because, most people that are crazy think they are normal. So, the fact that you think you are crazy means you are perfectly normal."

"So, have you been studying all this stuff?" I asked, amazed. He has never talked about any of this stuff before.

"It's not something I tell people about. They might think I am crazy," he said, smiling.

"Well, obviously I am not qualified to call you that, since I am hearing voices, seeing spirit hands, and talking to my dead dad." We both laughed.

"All right, shall we get this started? I am very curious what this spirit is trying to tell you."

"Okay, but I am going to get dressed, since we are not heading back to bed. You might want to think about it as well, since you might not be comfortable in your current attire either," I said, looking at him still in the nude.

"I am very comfortable," he said, laughing and posing for me. "But you're right, I should put something on, in case we get some company down here." After a few minutes, we went back downstairs. We started looking through the photographs. There were several pictures of Adam and me during the summers. Hardly any of Raylene. And even less of my mom. Most of them seemed to be my mom taking pictures of my dad. The next stack of photos were ones I took at some of the school events. Raylene riding in a float for the parade. The third stack was pictures my dad took of my mom while she was pregnant; she looked so happy.

"Well, that was all of it, there was nothing there that I could see."

"Well, that is confusing."

"I don't know, nothing here. We have looked through everything. I might have to wait to hear from it again."

"That is not recommended. Some spirits get pissed off if ignored. And this is the second time it has brought you here," Adam reminded me. He was right, it had led me here before.

"So, then what do we do? I don't know what it wants me to find."

"What were her exact words?"

"Just told me to check the drawer."

"Then I don't know, 'cause we did check all the drawers."

"So, I will risk the spirit getting mad, and wait for the next visit. Not that I am inviting her back."

"I don't know, Emily, from all the ghost movies that I have watched, they don't give up that easily. They stick around till their message is received."

"Great, a mysterious spirit, with a mysterious message of check the drawer. It must be some drawer for someone to come give me a message about it from beyond the grave."

"So, shall we go back to bed?" he said, grabbing me around the waist and pulling me close.

"Sure, not much more we can do about an invisible drawer," I said, kissing him. He pulled back.

"Invisible? Maybe not, but what about a false bottom?"

"Really?" I said, rolling my eyes, "So we have gone from supernatural spirit, to a spy movie with hidden drawers. What's next, hidden rooms and passageways?"

"It is worth checking, isn't it?"

"Fine, but for the record, the going to bed sounded like a much better idea," I whispered softly, closing the distance between our lips.

"Did I say check the drawer? I don't remember." He smiled.

"Too late, you brought it up, back to work."

"Remind me next time to keep my mouth shut." We went back into the dining room and checked the drawers again. Sure enough, the last drawer on the china cabinet had a board that could be removed. Underneath were letters. I grabbed them and we went back to the bedroom and lay in bed and began reading them.

They were from my dad to Raylene. He was explaining how sorry he was, and apologizing for how he acted when she first left, was the first three letters. Then, it seemed like she started writing back, he sounded more like he was answering questions and started asking them as well. I never knew they kept in touch. Dad kept writing about my life to her, and what I was up to. It usually had some reference to asking or wondering when she was going to move home. The letters were pretty regular for about two years and then stopped

"Why would these be hidden? Why did Dad not tell me he was in contact with her?" I asked, frustrated. "Why would someone want me to know about these and send a spirit to tell me about them?"

There was a crash from downstairs. Adam and I bolted out of bed.

"Why did you have to—" Ben yelled.

"Emily, Adam. I am sorry we woke you," Raylene said, interrupting Ben when she saw us at the bottom of the stairs. Ben ignored us and left the cabin. Raylene chased after him.

"Looks like no one is getting any sleep tonight," Adam said.

"Well, now that we found the letters and there is no danger of angry spirits, I think it is safe for us to," I said jokingly. Even as I said it, something didn't feel right. It didn't feel finished. But for tonight, it needed to be.

I knew deep down I would see the spirit again.

Chapter 8

There was more arguing the next morning between Raylene and Ben, and resulted in the same outcome of Ben storming off. Raylene didn't follow this time.

"You want to talk about it?" I asked, pouring a cup of coffee.

"Not much to talk about. He'll get over it."

"Okay, just thought I would ask. You were there for me with James."

"Thank you, but no." I could see she was uncomfortable. Maybe Ben didn't believe her about James and was pushing for answers. As much as I wanted to know, I would wait till it blew over. I didn't want to add to it.

"I found some letters Dad wrote to you," I said.

"Oh. Really, can I see them?" I went up to my room and grabbed them. "Wow these are so old, he started sending them a few months after I took off. Where did you find them?"

"In a drawer in the china cabinet."

"Cool, I'll have to re-read them at some point." I didn't want to make a big deal about it, but if she had been gone all this time and just got back into town, how would the letters have gotten here. Dad sent them to her, so she had them. But she also didn't know they were in the drawer, so it wasn't recently put there.

"So how fun was it travelling the world."

"It was good," she said quickly. There was something she didn't want to talk about. I wonder what happened. It seemed no matter what conversation I tried to talk to her about, after a few sentences, she would stop talking about it. Maybe she just wasn't in the mood to talk. I stopped trying and went to finish my coffee on the porch.

Before Adam left, he warned me about the rain. They were speculating that it would wash out the road to town.

"You want to come shopping with me?" I asked Raylene when I went back inside.

"We just went," she said, referring to her and Ben.

"Yeah, but we need to stock up. Adam said the rain tonight might take out the road to town. We might not be able to go in for a few days. I would like extra alcohol if that is going to happen."

"Oh, maybe Ben and I should just grab a hotel in town. I think that all of us here together might make us all a little stir-crazy if we can't leave."

"It is up to you, but the offer still stands if you want to come. I will be leaving in about an hour."

"Okay, thanks. I'll talk it over with Ben." I got cleaned up and dressed. Raylene decided not to come with me. As a precaution in case the rain took out the power, I decided to get a camping stove and extra canned food. Better to have it than not to, especially if the road did go out, no one would be able to come by to fix the power. I figured it probably wouldn't happen, and I was probably overreacting. I smiled to myself at the thought that Raylene would be nagging at me and telling me I was crazy, that we didn't need all this stuff. I stopped by Adam's work.

"So, will I see you tonight?" I asked when he finished with a customer.

"Yup."

"Good."

"Good?"

"Yeah, I wasn't sure if you would, seeing as how we could be stuck out there and you wouldn't be able to get back into town for work and stuff."

"Well, when you put it that way…definitely coming by," he said, smiling. "Stranded with you or working, there is no contest of where I would rather be."

"Won't your dad be upset?"

"Nah, he would want me to make sure you are safe. Anything can happen out there."

"So, are you saying you think I am in danger?"

"No, but like with the windows, and…"

"And?"

"Okay. Fine, you caught me. I was trying to make it sound like you would need me out there, but in all honestly, I can't seem to keep myself away from you," he said, slightly blushing.

"That is really nice to hear, Adam," I said, grinning.

"What's that look for?" I moved closer to him and whispered in his ear.

"I can't seem to stay away from you either." A little while later, I left and headed to the liquor store.

When I got back to the cabin, Raylene wasn't there. The rain started to drizzle while I carried in the groceries. By the time I finished, it was pouring. Adam, Raylene and Ben pulled up just as I was closing the last of the windows in the cabin. I was glad she didn't decide to stay in town. Hopefully, if she couldn't get away, I might be able to get some answers from her. And as I suspected, Raylene did think I was nuts when she saw all the groceries on the counter. Adam and Ben were on my side, better to be prepared. But I did see them smirking about it as well. We didn't even have enough room in the cupboards for all of it, we left some of the canned stuff in bags in the corner of the kitchen.

Raylene volunteered to make dinner. Adam and I realized we hadn't stocked up wood for the fire. We went to get the wood that was still on the front lawn. Even though it hadn't been raining that long, it was still too late to use the wood tonight, it was too wet.

We had to get changed when we were done, the dirt from the wood and all the rain meant we got covered in mud. At dinner, it didn't look like the problem between Ben and Raylene had been fixed, they were not talking to each other at all. No one was really talking about anything.

"What made you change your mind about staying in town?" I asked Raylene, as we sipped wine in the living room since the guys offered to do dishes.

"The main reason I guess is that we needed to work things out, so if we are here, it would be easier to work out. In town, we would have had a lot easier time avoiding each other."

"Is it that serious?" She looked at me and rolled her eyes. I could tell she didn't want to explain. Or maybe it was that I should have already known. Maybe it was about the James thing. She hasn't admitted it to me, but maybe she did to Ben. "Ray, please."

"Look, I can't. There is just too much."

"Then start at the beginning."

"I said no," she said, slamming down her wine glass on the coffee table, breaking the base of it, so the wine fell over and spilled. Upset at herself and me, she ran out of the room. I cleaned up the glass. Adam brought me some paper towel when he came into the room and saw me, while Ben went to look for Raylene.

"I don't know, why won't she tell me anything? It's only making her look more guilty."

"While your female counterpart may not be talking, Ben needed to talk, but I will tell you later." Great, why do people do that? I know a secret, but you can't know. It only makes a person want to know even more than they did before. I know he wanted to wait till Raylene and Ben had no chance of interrupting us, but it was still annoying. Maybe it was just this whole situation that was getting annoying. The not knowing if my sister actually slept with my boyfriend. Well, my ex-boyfriend. And if she did, then why would she?

Finally, when we were lying in bed, Adam decided to tell me what Ben talked to him about.

"So, he didn't go into a lot of detail, but he said there was more to this family tradition of yours."

"What? Wait, how would he know?"

"Raylene told him."

"Why wouldn't Dad tell me? Why wouldn't Raylene tell me?" I got out of bed, dressed, and went outside. It was still raining and getting worse. Did it matter that much that I wasn't told? I thought about it for a while. Yes, I guess it did. If it was something I was supposed to be doing and couldn't do it because I wasn't told. But then again, maybe I wasn't supposed to do the other part of the tradition. Maybe it was something just for Raylene, but what—

"Hey," Adam said, coming outside to join me.

"Hey." I moved closer to him when he sat beside me and he wrapped an arm around my shoulders.

"Feel like sharing?"

"I don't know. Everyone is lying and keeping secrets from me, and ordinarily, I don't think it would matter much, but whatever Ray is keeping from me is causing trouble between her and Ben, so it would have to be something really big."

"But really, is it that big? I mean, have you told her about the spirits? Or the dreams about your dad? You have your secrets too."

"Those are not really secrets, though; if she asked, I would tell her. Also, nothing affects Raylene, yet her secrets may have been with my cheating ex-boyfriend, and now, is creating problems all around her because no one is saying anything. And the more they try to hide it, the worse it feels."

"Granted, she is acting strange and avoiding conversations with you. Look, I understand things are weird right now, but it should make a little more sense when we go to my parents for dinner."

"Why don't you just tell me, since they obviously told you?"

"Because you won't believe me. You might, if you hear it from them." I rolled my eyes at him but left it alone; I could tell I wasn't going to get any more out of him.

"Emily," I heard my name being screamed from the dining room. I twisted in the seat to look inside the cabin window. Why was it so mad? I did what it asked.

"Stay here, Adam." I didn't want him there, so there were no distractions. I had to make sure this time, I would hear. The screaming of my name continued.

"What's going on?"

"It's back, and it is not happy."

"Then I should go—"

"No, I will be back as soon as I can," I stated firmly and ran as quickly as I could to where I heard my name being called.

"I'm here."

"Emily, you didn't look, you need to find it," the voice screamed; I had to cover my ears.

"I tried; I found the letters," I yelled back. *Crap, shouldn't have done that, Raylene and Ben might have heard.*

"Emily, check the drawer." And from the darkness, a ghostly hand reached into the cabinet, into one of the drawers. Suddenly, the hand was on my shoulder, shoving me. I tripped and hit my head on the corner of the cabinet. But I finally saw it. A latch under the lip of the bottom half of the cabinet. After making sure that no one had come down the stairs, I pulled it and out popped a small concealed drawer. I grabbed the contents and reclosed the drawer. I went to get Adam from outside and we went back to my room. Adam's look of concern alleviated when I told him what happened and I showed him what I had found. It was another packet of letters. They were the replies to Dad's letters.

"Crap, I knew I should have gone with you," he said, jumping up to take a look at my head when he saw the blood dripping from my forehead. Returning a couple minutes later with the first aid kit, he cleaned up the cut on my forehead and we sat down to read the letters.

Raylene and Dad wrote back and forth for years, and I never knew. The last letter Raylene wrote said she was moving back. Moving back where? Here? Has she been here all this time? The last ten years, she had been back? All the postcards that she mailed me?

"What are you going to do?" Adam asked after a while.

"Why would she lie? I don't understand. She had been back for ten years. Why would she not tell me she was back? What would be the purpose?" I was getting angry at her the more I thought about it. She obviously had forgiven Dad and come back, kept in touch with him. So, was she mad at me? Is that why she didn't tell me she was back?

"There could be another explanation," Adam said, as if he knew what I was thinking.

"Yeah, I would love to hear it."

"Maybe your dad told her not to tell you."

"That doesn't make sense, why would he do that?" He looked like he wanted to say much more. What was he not telling me? What was so important that he had to wait for his parents to tell me? And why I wouldn't believe him?

"You should get some sleep, maybe ask her tomorrow." Frustrated, I did as he said. I closed my eyes and let my mind drift. I drifted to my past. Raylene had just gotten back from a long walk in the forest behind the house. She looked sad; this was about a week before Raylene took off. It was the last days of summer and I was heading into the city soon, look at a few colleges that I was thinking about attending. That night, Dad was quiet while we ate dinner, and in the morning, when I woke up, Raylene and he were out in the boat on the lake. We had been drifting apart for a while before this happened, but this week seemed really hard on Raylene.

Come to think of it, that whole week, they were nearly inseparable; the more I thought about it, the sadder I saw Raylene get. At the time, I didn't notice. Did Dad see it? Was it Dad making her sad?

"You are still thinking about stuff, aren't you?" Adam asked.

"Yeah."

"Do you need some help getting to sleep?"

"Hmm, what are you offering?" I asked, opening one eye slightly to look at him.

"Roll over," he said. I did, and he began massaging by back. Wow, it felt so good, and he was right. I stopped thinking. My mind and body felt like mush. If anyone would have asked me anything, I would have answered yes to everything without knowing what was actually said.

The next morning, I awoke to shouting. Adam was not in bed. I ran to go see what was going on.

"Maybe you two need some space, take a breather," Adam said, almost shoving Ben out the door. It was still pouring rain outside.

"Ray, what's going on?"

"Nothing," she turned and yelled at me. With a look of regret she added, "Sorry, I didn't mean to snap at you. But really, it's nothing."

"Okay," I said, not convinced. I grabbed a coffee.

"I know you're trying to help, but really, it is just a disagreement. Every couple goes through it."

"Yeah, I get it. Look, this might not be the right time to ask this, but did Dad ever—"

"Did Dad what?"

"Well, last night, I remembered the week before you took off, you and Dad spent a lot of time together, and you seemed really sad. I was wondering if Dad...Okay, I'm just going to say it...Did Dad molest you?"

"Oh, my god. Emily, no."

"Oh, good," I said, relieved. I didn't really think Dad could do something like that, but I had to be sure.

"How could you think—?"

"I didn't. I just had to be sure."

"Why?"

"Like I said, you seemed so sad that last week and then left, and didn't talk to Dad much, so I guessed something happened, and I needed to make sure it wasn't that."

"No, it wasn't. You don't have to worry about that."

"Well…are you going to tell me what it was?"

"It was a long time ago; it doesn't matter now." I left her there and went out to check on the boys, bringing a coffee for both of them.

"Everything all right out here?" I asked, handing them each a cup.

"Will be when the rain stops," Adam said. Their discussion must not have gone well. I was getting frustrated again. No one was telling me anything, and okay, maybe some things were not my business, but this was getting ridiculous.

"Emily, are you okay?" Ben asked when he looked at me.

"Fine, why wouldn't I be?" He pointed at my forehead.

"What happened?"

"Ah, yeah. I didn't turn the light on last night and tripped. Just a bit clumsy lately, nothing serious." My plan to make light of the accident seemed to have the opposite effect on them. They looked almost worried.

Two days later, the rain finally stopped. I got to open the windows and let some fresh air in. Ben and Raylene kept their distance. If one entered the kitchen, the other would leave. Raylene told me they were supposed to work things out, but they seemed farther apart.

It took almost three more days for the roads to start draining enough water to make attempts at getting to town. Adam would check the roads regularly. The closer it got to the roads being passable, the more on edge everyone seemed. I had to stop pressing everyone on their behavior and their secrets just to make it bearable. Raylene was talking less and less, Ben was outside more and more. I didn't know what to do to make things better. Adam came home one day, letting me know that we could probably get to town tomorrow, and that we could go see his parents if I was up for it.

I can't say I didn't try to get out of going. I tried a few times. As much as I wanted to question them about the lore of the town, it felt weird to. I mean, they were Adam's parents, and what if they asked questions about us? I don't think I was ready to answer any of it. Adam made some valid points and I finally caved and agreed to go.

It was a simple meal, but very good. By the look of their home, they didn't need a lot of stuff. They were happy living simply. Adam's dad owned the hardware store where Adam worked. His mom was the local librarian. She loved books and did not hesitate to start in on the history of my parent's home, which Adam put a stop to till after dinner. Seated on the back porch with a glass of wine, Adam finally let her speak about what may be going on at the cabin.

"So, this town had 12 original families that built this town from the ground up. Yours was one of them. They each built a cabin." She paused. "How much do you believe in the supernatural?"

"I don't, not really, but I have come to have an open mind about it." I mean, how could I deny the screaming spirit calling my name or shoving me?

"Okay, well then, I will tell you what I know, and you can believe me or not." I nodded. I mean, how bad could it be? "Okay, so I don't have all the details on how this started or why, I only know after it changed everything for those 12 families. Their crops grew better, they lived longer, they were healthier—"

"How do you know that?"

"Journals from a couple of the families that have been willing to let me read them."

"Did all the families keep one?"

"I don't know. Most won't talk about it."

"Okay, go on."

"Well, the families generally were better off, as long as they followed the ritual. Now, Adam tells me you know of this."

"I thought I did. But now, I am not sure. I guess I only know part of it, my dad didn't really talk too much about it."

"Oh," she said, looking confused, then looking at Adam. "Her father chose the other one? I can't tell her, it won't be fair," she said, and quickly got up and left.

"Adam, what did she mean?" I asked, baffled. "What did my father choose? Was it between me and Ray and he chose her?"

"I'll go talk to her," he said and followed her in the house. Why did his mom call it a ritual and not a tradition? Ritual sounded more…

"There is a way for it to work. My brother and I did it," Adam's dad said from the shadows.

"What?"

"For you both, you…and your sister."

"I don't understand."

"You will," he said, and disappeared into the darkness. Why was everyone so cryptic? Why couldn't they just say what they meant instead of passing it off to others and expecting the next person to tell me what the hell was going on? I tried to wait patiently for Adam to convince his mom to tell me the secret lore about the cabins.

I screamed as a dog that was twice my size bolted up to me and jumped in my lap. He came out of nowhere. His tongue lapped the side of my face. I tried to push him off of me and his nails dug in and scratched my leg. I screamed, again pushing him even more. Who was I kidding, this dog was unmovable, unless he wanted to.

"Get off," I yelled, squirming under his weight, trying to pull myself out from under him. I could feel the blood from the wound running down my leg.

"Here, boy," I heard a man calling. The dog decided to listen and trotted off to the voice that called him. I made my way inside, calling for Adam.

"Hey, we were just coming out—" he trailed off when he saw my leg. Adam took me to the washroom and helped me get cleaned up.

"How long?" his mom asked, coming around the corner, watching as Adam cleaned and bandaged the wound.

"Since her sister showed up," Adam replied.

"Nothing before?"

"No."

"What are you guys talking about?" I said, getting annoyed.

"Finish cleaning her up and I will tell her." Adam nodded and we joined her in the living room. "This is not my place to tell you," she said, seriously. "And I don't know what the consequences are for what I am about to do, but my son has asked that you know." I looked at him and he smiled slightly. She continued, "I also realize that by telling you, I am going against your father's wishes."

She was really starting to creep me out but I kept silent.

"Your injuries have been increasing since your sister arrived?"

"Yes."

"And how 'bout your fear? What you would have brushed off normally has been slowly getting worse?"

"Yes."

"Okay, so the lore goes back, way back to when the original cabins were built. The warning to only have one child."

"Why?"

"Again, I don't have the complete details. All the journals would need to be found and read to get the whole story of how and why. It is only said that one child survives from each of the families to inherit the cabin. Usually, it is the one that knows the full history which, in this case, would be your sister."

"So, you're telling me I am going to die?"

"If my son hadn't convinced me to tell you, yes, you would have. He is hoping that me telling you would prevent this."

"But if I change things and survive, what will happen to Ray?" I asked, looking from her to Adam.

"It will be okay, you'll see," he said, squeezing my hand. But I also noticed he avoided answering my question.

"And me getting hurt has something to do with this?"

"It is one of the signs, yes," she said, continuing. "For the sake of making this easier, I will use you as the one that won't survive." I was about to object but I could see her point. Raylene knew all along about this and I was only finding out now. "The ritual starts when the handcrafted item, made by two people, gets added to the house, and gets engaged. This part, Adam tells me, you knew."

"Yes."

"After it begins, it's extremely hard to stop. The other sibling who is not part of the ritual starts getting injured, sick, everything in their lives starts going wrong. Almost like you have eternal bad luck, this process will continue till your death." I could feel my eyes start to bulge out of my head.

"How long?"

"Usually, it is a few weeks after the wedding. A fatal accident will occur at the cabin. Most of the time unexplainable."

"How do you know all this? This is crazy."

"As I said, I have read a couple of the original journals. I have also seen it happen a couple of times."

"You said it was hard to stop. But not impossible. How would I stop it?" Adam and his mom looked at each other.

"You would need to kill the ones who have started the ritual."

"No," I said, standing up. "There has to be another way. Adam…your dad and uncle are both alive. They found a way."

"Yes, they did but that was because my dad married into my mom's family, and Mom was an only child. So, my uncle got to keep the original family cabin and my dad now belongs to this one."

"So, I would have to marry into one of the other 11 families to live?"

"Yes, just like we are asking Adam to do. So, his sister can live."

"Is that what you were wanting from me? You were trying to get me to marry you? Conveniently, James died, so that wasn't a problem but with my sister showing up and her being the one chosen, it screwed things up," I yelled at him. "Take me home now." I stormed out of the house. I would have preferred walking with how I was feeling but with my leg the way it was, I knew I wasn't going to make it.

Adam tried to explain a few times on the way home. I wouldn't listen. I was furious. He pulled up to the house. I jumped out of the truck and stormed into the cabin. I heard the squealing tires as he left.

"Is everything okay?" Raylene asked from the dining room.

"Does it matter?"

"Of course it does, you're my sister."

"Really? Well, you don't act like it. You sleep with my boyfriend; you won't talk to me unless it suits you. And now, I just found out that you have been lying to me this whole time and didn't tell me that I am going to die." She went ghastly white.

"Dad said you wouldn't find out. It was never supposed to be like this."

"Like what?"

"I did move back, when the letters stopped. He knew it would be easier on me if we stayed apart and not had a sister relationship. Dad kept tabs on you and would let me know what was going on with you. Eventually, Dad told me you were with James. I was so happy for you when you found someone. But Dad said you were getting too close to getting engaged from the discussions he had with you and that it would ruin everything. He told me I needed to, so you would break up with him, so I listened to him. You didn't find out about the first two times, so I waited, hoping. And then Dad died, and I thought…or rather, didn't think. I was so mad that he would put me in that situation. But I did it again. Only, you didn't break it off when you found out. You forgave him. When I learned that he didn't want to see me again 'cause he was getting engaged to you, I only wanted to keep him from meeting you that night, so he wouldn't ask you. I never meant it to get that far. I didn't want to hurt you but I needed it to stop." She was bawling as she told me.

"So, instead, you now have reversed it so that I die. Thank you so much for that. At least I didn't know. You did it on purpose. Not only have you fucked up a relationship, but now, you are willing to kill me. Why couldn't you tell me, and we could have found a way out of this together?"

"I couldn't. There are consequences to tell anyone who wasn't—"

"Chosen, yeah." I couldn't believe Dad chose.

"Are you mad?"

"Yes, I am mad at all of you. I can't believe this. This is all so crazy."

"Well, maybe you could talk to Adam—"

"No," I yelled, interrupting her. "He is the last person I want to talk to. I never want to talk to him again."

"What happened?"

"No, you still have a lot of explaining to do before I trust you again. But I have had enough for tonight. I need to go to bed." As I entered my room, I locked my door. Not that I really needed to. It was only a matter of time. If she wanted me dead, she just had to finish the ritual.

"Emily," I heard the whisper through the door. It woke me out of my sleep.

"Emily," I heard again, and watched as the lock on the door flipped open. I got out of bed and opened the door. The voice now came from the bottom of the stairs.

"Emily," it called for the third time, and I followed. The whispering spirit led me to my father's grave, and before I knew it, I was yelling and screaming at his grave. How could he choose? How could any parent make a choice like that, and why did he choose her? Did I do something wrong? I didn't notice the blood on my hands from hitting and punching the ground. I screamed and cried.

"Dad, why? I need to know." There was no answer. I laid down, resting my head near where his head may have been.

"It has you both now," I heard my dad say.

"Why did you choose her? Not that I wanted you to choose me, or either of us, but I need to know, why?"

"I have no good explanation. I loved you both, your mom didn't want to choose. I had to make the decision on my own."

"How did you choose? Was it a heads or tails, flip of a coin? Which daughter lives?" I yelled at the ground.

"No. Look, I can't explain why I chose the way I did."

"The consequence is death. That is why Ray didn't tell me."

"Yes."

"And Adam's mom? Will she die too, for telling me?"

"Yes."

"Dad, where is the journal? She said all the families probably had one. If she is giving up her life for me, I would like to give her something too. She has invested a lot of time into figuring all this out."

"I buried it, where your mom is supposed to be. Emily, just so you know, I was going to tell you."

"And that is why you are lying here."

"Yes. Don't be too hard on Adam. He has been in love with you since you were kids. You know that. The other thing is just secondary. He didn't even find out about any of this till recently."

"Emily, what happened?" Raylene and Ben were rushing up to me, yelling.

"I got mad," I said. My hands had crusty dried blood on them, they hurt when I moved them.

"Let's get you inside, you are freezing."

"No, I have something I need to do. Leave me alone." I turned to her and glared.

"Okay, let us know if you need anything." They left me at the graves.

While I dug at mom's grave, I was trying to figure out what the spirit I kept seeing was doing. Why did it want me to know all this? It led me to the letters, which has now caused a bigger rift between Ray and I, and it wanted me to talk with Dad. There were parts of me that were starting to doubt the conversations I had with him were all in my head. How would I have known he buried the journal here? I don't remember seeing him do it. So, if it was no longer a dream, then who was I talking to? Could it really be him? No. Maybe. But if not, then how? Who?

I was just about to give up thinking I was crazy and made all this shit up when the shovel hit something. I dug around it and pulled up a lock box. So, when Dad buried the box for mom's grave, it was this, not a casket box. I grabbed my car keys hanging on the wall and drove to Adam's house. As I was getting out, I realized I probably should have dressed better and cleaned myself up. I knocked on the door. It was too late now. I was already here.

"Is your mom here?" I asked, when Adam answered the door. He led me to the kitchen where she was making breakfast.

"I wanted to apologize for the way I stormed out of here yesterday. I know what it cost you to tell me. I am sorry. If I would have known."

"Don't. It was my choice. I told you I didn't know what it would cost me, but I did. Any mother would do what she can to save her children."

"I can't repay you for what you have done, but I did want to bring you this," I said, giving her the box. Adam went to get bolt cutters and cut the lock off the box.

A big smile spread across her face when she saw it. It was a leather-bound book, very worn. There was a leather lace tied around the book.

"How did you find it?" Adam asked.

"My dad told me," I said, looking at him. "I was going to ask, have you ever heard of a spirit helping someone in my situation?" I asked, looking at Adam's mom.

"A spirit?"

"Yes, it keeps calling me, showed me letters, led me to my dad last night, who told me where to find that."

"Honestly, I can't say. This is the first time I am hearing about it." Adam avoided looking at me, but noticed my hands.

"Emily, what happened?" he said, panicked.

"I was frustrated and took it out on the ground." He smirked. He left and came back with supplies and started cleaning them up.

"That's okay. It seems to be wanting to help me, so I guess that is a good thing. Hopefully this helps with putting more of it together."

"Do you want to stay and read it?" she asked.

"No, Adam can bring it back to me when you are done."

"Thank you," she said, grateful. When Adam finished wrapping up my hands, he walked me out.

"Why would you get your mom to sacrifice herself like that?"

"All parents do it."

"But your mom didn't have to. They told you, but gave you the loophole, so they wouldn't have to tell your sister the bad side of it."

"She chose to; I asked her to."

"Why?"

"You already know the answer to that," he said, looking deep into my eyes. I felt heat rising to my cheeks. "My mom wanted to do this for me."

"What about your dad?"

"He told you there was a way to survive for both of you, didn't he? He was trying to let you know that it didn't have to be set in stone."

"Adam, I can't kill Ray, and they have already started the ritual."

"I know, but there may be more than one way to stop this."

"I have to go, come by when your mom is done with the book. In the meantime, I have more to discuss with Ray. She finally admitted she slept with James trying to break us up," I said, sitting in the car.

"That is pretty bad."

"Anyway, I really need t—" I couldn't finish my sentence. Adam had stuck his head through the window and pressed his lips on mine.

"Sorry, I don't know if that was okay or not, with how mad you were, but—"

"Adam, it's okay," I said, blushing. "Bye."

Back at the cabin, I showered and changed. Bruises were forming, peeking out from the top of the bandages that Adam had wrapped on my hands. I cleaned and re-bandaged the wound on my leg. Ben and Raylene were sitting in the kitchen when I walked in there.

"How much have you told Ben of what's going on?"

"All of it. It is why we have been arguing."

"Did he know about James?"

"Yes. The arguing has more been about how long to put off the wedding."

"Oh, and did you guys decide?"

"Not yet, but the last day to do it will be the day before my 30th birthday."

"I see."

"I thought we should wait, till you and Adam decided to get together. Then you could move in there," Ben said.

"Yeah, well, that isn't going to happen, so don't wait for that."

"Why? You two are good together," Raylene said.

"Yeah, well, he has a sister, and his parents want her to have the cabin."

"Oh."

"Why couldn't you just wait before adding your item and getting engaged? You knew James and I were through, or mostly through. You had to know I wouldn't accept that he cheated on me again. Why did you have to start it?" I asked her.

"I couldn't take that chance. I stayed away from you for years, so I could do what I needed to do when the time came. If the situation were reversed, what would you have done? Could you have let me go through with it, knowing that outcome for you?"

"I don't know. And we will never know, 'cause I never had the choice. I know that Dad was planning on telling me, which is why he is dead, and maybe Mom wanted the same thing. When I talked to Dad, he said Mom couldn't make the choice. They wanted both of us to know."

"You talked to Dad again?"

"I don't know, it is not really him. But that is not the issue. If they wouldn't want to go through with it, how could you?"

"Easy for them, they were our parents. They loved us. For most of my life, I was told to distance myself from you. Maybe if we grew up together the whole time, it would be different. And it is not like I knew they were trying to stop this, up until I left, and for all those years separated from you, Dad kept telling me I had to do this."

"Maybe you're right." I couldn't help but feel how cold she was being about this. She could use the distancing as an excuse all she wanted, but I didn't buy it. There was still something she was not telling me. "What I don't understand is if all these families know about the consequences of having more than one child, why have more than one? Adam's mom never had to deal with it 'cause she was an only child." Raylene looked at me as if having a revelation.

"You're right, this isn't the first generation, so they knew. Why would they put their kids through this?" Great, I gave her a new excuse of why it was not her fault. Maybe I would get Adam to ask his mom for me. There had to be a reason. Maybe someone did try it.

Chapter 9

A few days later, Adam showed up after dinner. He came by to return the book. I apologized for the way I reacted when I found out and invited him inside. Ben and Raylene had gone out for the evening. They were grateful that the rain hadn't returned and kept the road clear, they had been using any excuse to take a drive into town.

Adam and I sat, quietly sipping wine in front of the fireplace. I mentioned the sibling thing to Adam.

"I don't know. I can ask Mom."

"By the way, your mom was the only child, how did her parents swing that."

"I don't know too much. I just know that her mom died."

"That must have been hard on your mom."

"Yeah, anyway, any more spirits or dad visits?" I shook my head.

"If they wanted me to know, now I know. I don't know what good it does. Ray and Ben are still engaged, and as soon as they are married, my days are numbered."

"Do you think there is any way to split them up? Now that both of you know. Maybe you can both stay single. I realize it is not the most ideal situation, but under the circumstances."

"I don't know, maybe. But wouldn't there be a contingency somewhere? If there is one for people telling someone who wasn't chosen, there has to be one for not marrying."

"I don't know, it was just a thought. My only other thought was to split them up and see if any of the other families have someone available for her to marry."

"I can ask Ray if Dad told her any specifics about any of this."

"I will ask my mom too. Maybe she read something in one of the journals." He looked at me and smiled. Ben and Raylene walked in, arguing again.

"Don't bother," Ben said. "I'll sleep in town." He grabbed a change of clothes and tripped coming down the stairs. He grabbed the railing, dropped the clothes in his hands, and his legs shot out from underneath him. One foot got caught in the railings and twisted it. So not only was the bannister broken, he severely sprained his ankle. Adam called the doctor while Raylene and I tried to dislodge Ben's foot from the twisted angle he had it in. Limping, with each of us under one of his arms, we helped him back to bed.

"Why? Why would the house do that to him?" I asked Adam when we were alone.

"The house?"

"You know what I mean. I'm the one with the bad luck. Weren't Ray and Ben supposed to have good health and all that stuff from doing the ritual?"

"Now he is the one with the bad luck, is that what you think?"

"Well, what else?"

"Emily, accidents happen."

"You don't think it is strange? They have been fighting a lot, and now this. I mean, we were just talking about splitting them up, could the house be breaking them up?"

"Why are you blaming the cabin?"

"Because everything points to the cabin having a mind of its own. If you add a piece of yourself to the cabin, it owns you. That is what Dad says. That it is too late for Ray and me. It has already decided."

"And so?"

"So, what if instead of going with what Dad decided, the house is choosing me? It sent the spirits. It wants you and me to live."

"Why would you think that?"

"Because you gave me the music box that I made, and you finished before Ray showed up."

"Emily, I think this is going to your head. The house doesn't choose. Our parents choose."

"And who is the ritual for?" I looked at him quizzically. "Rituals are always for someone, so who benefits?"

"I don't know," he said, looking away.

"Either way, this all sounds insane, just like the thoughts in my head that Ben damaged the cabin, so now it is going to kill him when it gets the chance."

"Emily?"

"I know. Nuts, right?"

"Yeah, and you shouldn't talk like that."

"I know, but is it wrong for me to hope a little? I don't want to die."

"I guess I can understand that. I don't have to worry for a little bit. My sister doesn't want to settle down yet."

"Good, 'cause you might have to find someone else. I might not be around."

"Emily, what is with you tonight, you are talking—"

"Crazy…" I said, interrupting him. He didn't need to say it. I heard what I was saying, but I couldn't help myself.

"Come on, let's get you to bed."

"Not yet. I have to fix the bannister post."

"It is late, we can put it back together tomorrow."

"Adam, you told me not to anger the spirit. If the house is alive," I whispered, "don't you think it would want to be put back together tonight?" I could see the hesitation in his eyes whether to believe me or not, but he gave in and humored me.

"Okay, so no angry spirits, no angry cabin. No angry Emily."

"Exactly," I said, smiling. It was weird; I almost felt drunk, but I only had one glass of wine. Fixing it was easy, since Adam had his truck fully loaded with tools. Then, he helped me into bed.

"Stay with me," I said, grabbing his hand as he tried to leave.

"I shouldn't, you don't seem well."

"I am perfectly fine," I said seriously, "I just feel a little drunk."

"All the more reason for me not to stay."

"All the more reason for you to stay, in case I do some sleepwalking or see spirits. I need you to make sure I am not walking into the middle of the lake chasing after a butterfly."

He laughed.

"Well, when you put it that way," he said, smirking, climbed into bed beside me, and held me close, as I drifted off to sleep.

"Emily, Emily," I heard Raylene screaming, panicked. Adam and I rushed to the door.

"What's wrong?" Adam asked.

"Ben, I can't find him. I have looked everywhere. His car is here, but he isn't."

We scrambled to put clothes and shoes on. Since Raylene searched the house, we figured he must be outside. We found him on the dock with one leg in the water.

"Ben, I've been looking all over for you," Raylene said, running up to him.

"I've been around."

"You all right?" Adam asked.

"Not really sure. Do you think I could swim with my ankle the way it is, or would I drown?"

"All the more reason to not be here," Raylene said.

"I should be here. This is where I need to be," Ben replied calmly.

"Ben, you are acting strange. Please come back inside," she pleaded. "I'll make you breakfast."

"Not hungry. Hey, look, a butterfly," Ben said, and next thing I knew, he was in the water. Adam dove in after him before I knew what was happening.

"Oh my god, Ben, what were you thinking?" Raylene screamed, as Adam dragged him to the shore. I ran inside to get towels. They were halfway back to the cabin when I came back out. All I could think about was what I had told Adam last night, ending up in the lake, chasing a butterfly.

"Emily," Ben said, as they laid him on the bed.

"Yeah?"

"He wants you; I am only in the way." And then, he passed out. I couldn't help but wonder if he had been asleep the whole time. Who was the he? James had mentioned it too, but I thought he meant Adam. This was different; I was with Adam now. And how was Ben in the way of us being together? Unless he meant the being alive part, since Raylene and him were going through with the wedding.

"That was not Ben," Raylene said. "What is going on?"

"I don't know. Adam, would your mom know anything?"

"I could ask." He changed into dry clothes and said he'd be back later.

"What was the argument about?" I asked.

"What?"

"Last night. Why did he want to leave?"

"What are you asking about this for after what just happened?"

"Because that is what started all this," I said, raising my voice. "I am trying to figure out why he is hurt and acting the way he is, and it started last night. So, answer the question."

"Fine, jeez. He wanted to call off the wedding. He thought we should wait till we found a way out for you."

"But you said he knew all about this before, why did he change his mind? He was okay with letting me die before."

"Yeah, well, I guess he didn't think he would care, but then he met you and now actually watching you get hurt repeatedly…Anyway, now, he doesn't want to."

"Did Dad say anything about it? If…once the ritual was started, what would happen if it was stopped?"

"No, he never said. I guess he didn't think I needed to know. Do you think that is why he is acting crazy?" There was that word again, crazy. Is the cabin making us crazy, was any of this really happening? I wished in that moment that I had never come back. What was wrong with me? I don't believe in the supernatural, why couldn't I come up with a logical explanation of what was happening? My head was spinning. Almost like a bad hangover. I went to go lay down. Raylene said she would stay and watch over Ben to make sure he didn't do a repeat performance.

I woke up later that day to Adam kissing my forehead.

"Hey," I said, smiling up at him, rubbing my eyes. "Did your mom have any information?"

"No, from the journals she has read, this is a unique situation. How are you feeling?"

"I have a headache, maybe I should get some coffee. How is Ben? He was almost acting like James when he got sick, without the violence."

"I can go check on him. We won't let anything happen to him." I nodded and went to get coffee. Adam joined me in the kitchen and let me know Ben and Raylene were both sleeping.

"You don't think he was purposely trying to drown this morning, do you? He was sleepwalking or something, right?"

"It is possible, I guess. I couldn't help but notice a similarity to what you said last night."

"Yeah, I noticed it too. But, Adam, it wasn't the first time…"

"What do you mean?"

"It's happened before…with James. I didn't think anything much of it at the time, but now with Ben, I…maybe I caused it to happen too."

"I don't remember you saying anything about James."

"I didn't say it in front of anyone, but I was so mad at him."

"So, what? You imagined a piece of glass going through his head?"

"Oh, god, no, nothing like that. I just may have been stating very loudly that I wished I didn't have to see him ever again."

"Emily, I don't think that was your fault. He punched the wood and the glass fell. But maybe for the time being, maybe try not making any more comments like that," Adam said, concerned.

"You do think I had something to do with it?"

"No, but you have to admit it is quite a coincidence."

"Okay." I sipped my coffee. "How is your mom doing?"

"She has a bit of time, no urgent worry."

"Does she know how long?" Adam shook his head. I rubbed the back of my neck. Man, my head hurt.

"So, I didn't want to bring it up in case you got mad at me again, but how did you find out I wasn't just using you?"

"Dad told me."

"Yeah, I thought it would be something like that. Your dad liked to smooth things over if people had problems. He didn't like anyone arguing."

"You know, now that you mention it, I do remember that. How funny that you would remember something like that."

"I told you, your dad and I talked a lot. He almost felt like a second dad to me."

"Oh, were you able to ask your mom why the 12 families didn't stop having kids after the first one, so they didn't have to make the choice?"

"As far as she could tell, most of the time, the second child was never planned. She doesn't know how it was for all the families, but it seems that for the most part, it was accidental."

"But your mom was an only child."

"Yeah, her mom died in childbirth of the second child, the baby didn't make it."

"Oh, that is awful. So, we have a spirit trying to help somehow. A cabin that is alive and wants people to die. The more I say it out loud, the more ridiculous this whole thing seems."

"I don't really think the cabin is alive, and even if it was, why would it want blood?" I looked at Adam curiously.

"I didn't say it wanted blood. I said it wanted death, why else would the second sibling not chosen get bad luck and die every time?"

"There is no proof of that. It is just what my mom said the history was. Stories get embellished as they get passed down."

"Yet, all of them have died. Even you have said that it has already started with me. With me getting hurt all the time now."

"Coincidence."

"You were the one who started all this with telling me to listen to the spirits and taking me to talk to your mom. Why are you all of a sudden not believing that it could happen, and the cabin is alive? This has only started because of adding the music box and the picture frames to the house. Raylene and I never had any of this happen before."

"You're right, this is too crazy. I can't believe it. There has to be some other explanation," Adam said, trying to get off the topic. I grabbed my head again.

"Something is wrong. Check on Ben please," I said urgently. Adam didn't ask why, he bolted up the stairs. When the pain in my head lessened, I realized it was the cut on my head that was aching. And as I passed the cabinet to head upstairs, the place where I had hit it had no blood. I didn't clean it up, I thought to myself. Maybe Adam did? But he didn't know where I hit my head. I made my way upstairs to find Adam sitting on the floor next to Ben. There was blood pooling on the floor. The wall was dripping with blood as well. Raylene was asleep in bed.

"Call the doctor," Adam said frantically.

I grabbed the phone from his pocket. Adam was trying to keep pressure on the wound on Ben's head.

"Raylene," he kept calling, she didn't wake up. When I got off the phone, I ran to get towels to put over Ben's head. Then shook Raylene to try and get her to wake up.

"What? Whe—" she stopped and screamed. Jumping out of bed, she slipped on the blood and landed on the floor. "Oh, Ben, oh my god. What?" She struggled getting the words out through her sobs.

By the time the doctor got there, Ben was dead. He called the police. I didn't know what to do. I didn't know how to comfort Raylene. Both she and Adam sat on the floor next to Ben, covered in his blood.

The police arrived, took our statements, asked for next of kin. Raylene said he didn't have any that she knew of. It was weird that they were only thinking this was an accident. They didn't think that we did it. But then I saw Adam talking to the chief and realized, he was one of the twelve families. He knew exactly what was going on and was covering up the truth. Not that we killed Ben, but he was going to cover up the other truth by not bringing us in as suspects.

They took the body away; the cops left. I helped Raylene into the shower to clean off the blood. Then helped her into bed in the other guest room. The doctor left sedatives for her in case she needed them to sleep. I gave her one and waited for her to drift off to sleep.

I found Adam cleaning up the blood and helped him. We didn't talk. Really, what was there to say? Ben was dead. James was dead. Adam's mom was going to die. All because of some stupid tradition. Why? I couldn't understand why so many deaths would be worth good health. There had to be more to it. Who started this ritual?

I started the laundry to wash all the bloodied clothes and towels. Adam showered first, I followed after. He went to sleep. I grabbed the journal and read in front of the fireplace.

May 17th

The mass suicide of the Hellanger family got us an empty home, another family moved in down the way. They agreed, as the rest of us did. Was such an easy trap. What wouldn't we do for someone we loved? We never thought what it would mean for the future when we made the agreement. Maybe we should have.

August 9th

The Wilson's gave birth to a second child. They will be the first of us to suffer the burden. We really should have thought about this more. It seemed so easy to decide at the time. But as the time comes closer, I am having my doubts. So is my wife.

December 24th

We ate heartily this year. The town is expanding nicely. Maybe this wouldn't be so bad after all.

February 2nd

We were foolish, the first life taken. He didn't follow the rules. The rules were simple, he didn't listen. We should have thought harder about the future generations and what this agreement would mean to them. Our choice was wrong, but it is too late.

September 30th

My wife gave birth to our second child. How I wish they would not have to deal with our arrogance. We tried to cheat in life and we are paying for it in death.

"Emily?" Raylene called from the kitchen.

"Yes?"

"Why? We did what we were supposed to do."

"I don't know, Ray. I'm trying to find out. Our family started this journal. I'm hoping it has something in here." She snatched it out of my hands and started to read. I wasn't going to say anything, if she could find some closure from reading it, she could read it first.

I made her something to eat. Hours passed. She continued reading. I went to bed. Adam wrapped his arms around me as I climbed into bed.

What was going to happen now?

Chapter 10

When I woke up, Adam wasn't there. Raylene had fallen asleep on the couch, the embers were dying out in the fireplace. I put a couple more logs on and went to make some soup.

"So, now is your chance," Raylene said, coming in the kitchen.

"For what?"

"To save Adam and you from the fate I was going to condemn you to."

"No, I won't do that to you."

"Why not? I did it to you."

"We both know now, there is no reason to push it further. There doesn't have to be another ritual, or wedding. It can end here." She smiled. She looked so sad. Is that even possible, how can a smile be sad?

"Okay." For now, at least this can be put to rest. I didn't know if it would last or for how long she would pretend she wouldn't go through with it. But just from that one word, I could tell she would try again. I had to finish reading the journal.

June 1ˢᵗ

How do I choose? I never thought I would actually have to make the choice. I was naïve to think this day could be postponed indefinitely. I would not do what the Wilsons did. They told both and it ended in a blood bath, with one victor.

Will that happen with Raylene and me?

September 3ʳᵈ

My wife and I chose. I hope we chose correctly, and I will not ask for forgiveness. To my future generations, if you are ever reading this, who will all also have to make this choice, I am sorry. I couldn't lose her. I hope you understand I just never realized the price would be so high. In the moment, I thought anything was worth it. But now I see how terribly wrong I was.

October 12th

My wife could not live with the choice; she took her life today. The children didn't know why; I can't explain it to them. I still need to tell my oldest the rules.

I didn't want to keep reading, but I knew I had to.

April 7th

I finally told my eldest about the ritual, the rules.

- *Must do before the age of 30.*
- *Only one child will be spared.*
- *Can't tell sibling.*
- *Can't tell second child.*
- *If tell anyone outside family, will forfeit life.*
- *Spouse may be told only after getting engaged.*
- *If don't trust to keep secret, do not tell till after married.*
- *Any deviation means everyone dies.*

"So, what do you think now?" she asked, coming up behind me.

"I still won't do it," I said sincerely. Raylene was going to be 30 in a couple months. She didn't have a lot of time.

"I guess I could always try one of the other 11 families, see if they have any single guys not married." I couldn't understand her. It has been less than 24 hours since Ben died, and she was already thinking about finding someone. But then again, didn't I do the same thing with James? Not really, maybe, in some ways, but we were drifting apart for a while and I broke up with him and moved on before he died.

"So, what happens now?" I asked.

"I don't know, I will let you know." I nodded. I didn't want to push her right now. I looked around the cabin.

"So, what have you been up to since you weren't really travelling?"

"Oh, I have been travelling, but only for vacations. A couple weeks at a time."

"You had the money for that?"

"Yeah. I worked when I needed to, saved up, picked a spot, came back, and worked again."

"What was your favorite place you went to?"

"Greece, the island of Crete was breathtaking."

"Emily," a voice whispered. I saw a shadow move behind Raylene. I pretended not to notice, so Raylene wouldn't get suspicious. Last thing I needed was for Raylene to think I was crazy.

"So, what are your plans for the day?"

"I was thinking about taking the boat out, we have had so much rain, haven't been able to enjoy the lake much this summer. You?"

"I'm going to read more of the journal," I said.

"Okay, have fun." She left the room quickly.

"Can you try to keep this to when I am alone, please? It is weird enough listening to someone who isn't there."

"Emily," the voice whispered again and touched me on the shoulder, which made me jump backward. Last time it touched me, it knocked me into the china cabinet. I didn't relish the idea of it being able to touch me.

"What?" I yelled.

"Emily, who are you talking to?" Raylene asked.

"Oh, no one, myself, I guess. Umm, I thought you left."

"Yeah, just grabbing some snacks," she said, looking at me strangely.

"Just curious, did you originally push me into getting into the relationship with Adam 'cause you thought I could move in with him and it would work out for both of us?" She shifted her eyes slightly to look behind me. I followed her eyes, but saw nothing.

"What? Oh, umm, yeah. I have to go into town, I just remembered. I was going to pick up something." She returned the snacks to the kitchen and bolted out of here like the house was on fire. I couldn't help but wonder if she was hearing or seeing the spirits too.

"Okay, she's gone," I said. Nothing. "I'm listening." Again, nothing. "Okay, well, you know where to find me when you are ready to talk." I sat back on the couch and started reading more of the journal.

At some point, the original writer stopped writing and someone else took over. They wrote down their experiences with the other families and the ritual, and how it affected him and his wife. How hard it was for them to watch their one son deteriorate and get mentally destroyed, till he took his own life. Three others kept the story going, all telling of the gruesome tragedies that happened to their children, wives, brothers, sisters. None of them found a way out. I got to the last entry. There was only one, written by my father. It was a little over a year before my mom died when this entry was made.

July 24th

What have I done? I am watching the relationship between the two, change. Raylene is pulling away from Emily. It is breaking my heart to watch this, but it has to be done. My wife is no longer speaking with me. What else could I do? I begged her to understand. I made the choice, so she wouldn't have to. I told Raylene, so she wouldn't have to.

I was so engrossed in the journal; I hadn't even noticed when Adam showed up. When he called my name from the kitchen, I jumped out of my seat.

"Yeah," I said, breathing heavily.

"I was wondering what you wanted for dinner."

"Oh, um, anything."

"Is it that good?"

"No, it gives details on what the siblings who didn't complete the ritual went through. It is disgusting and scary to think that I will have to go through this."

"You technically don't have to," he said, looking at me.

"Adam, no, I told you I am not killing my sister. I can't. I can't let her suffer like these people did," I said, holding up the book.

"What if she was willing to do it for you?"

"That would be her choice, but I can't. I think that is why Dad had the book buried, so neither of us could read what would happen to the other. That it would be our choice."

"Well, your sister wants to go ahead with it."

"Maybe, hopefully, in the next two months, we can find something to stop this. And currently, I don't think she has any prospects, though she mentioned checking out the other families to see if anyone was available." He shifted his eyes away from looking at me.

"She came to see me in town today."

"Oh?" I asked questioningly.

"Yeah, she said she had a proposal for me, literally."

"She proposed?"

"Yeah, she said it would take care of both our problems. Mine for not having a place once my sister decides to marry, and hers."

"Oh." I was shocked, and hurt that she would do it again. First James, now Adam. "What did you say?" I asked, not wanting to look at him.

"Really? Do you actually have to ask?" he asked me.

"How do I know what you want? Ray only wants to save her ass and either of us would work for you to live."

"Emily, I wasn't even tempted to accept her offer." I couldn't help but smile a little. He came over and gave me a kiss. "Okay?"

"Okay."

"All right, I'm going to let you get back to your journal. I'll make some dinner."

"Okay." He left the room.

"So, he decided to blame it on me, did he?" Raylene said, coming out of the shadows.

"Ray? I didn't know you were back."

"Yeah, we got back at the same time," she said, coming to start the fire in the fireplace in front of me. "He didn't tell you the whole truth, Emily."

"Yeah, I went to see him. To see if he knew anyone that was available, or if he knew of any way out of this. He and I getting married was his idea," she said.

"I thought we agreed not to do this."

"I know, that is what I told him." She stared at me as if that would help make me believe her. Honestly, her track record for telling me the truth hasn't been the best.

"Dinner is...Hey, Raylene, dinner is ready." His eyes shifted between the two of us.

"Great, I am hungrier than I thought I was," I said, jumping up and dashing to the kitchen as fast as possible. Dinner was quiet. No one said a word. Raylene disappeared right after dinner. While cleaning up the dishes, Adam asked if I believed him or Raylene.

"You, of course. Ray has been lying to me since she took off after graduation, why would I believe her." He seemed relieved.

Later that night, as we lay in bed, I remembered the spirit from that afternoon. It hadn't come back. Did I make it mad by not responding to it? I told Adam about it when he asked what I was thinking about. He let me know that spirits come and go, they couldn't hang around. It would be back.

"They are lying to you," I heard a voice whisper from the dark corner of the room.

"Who?" I asked. That was a stupid question. I knew the answer before I asked it.

"Downstairs." I did as the voice asked, checking to make sure that Adam was still asleep.

"Up there," I heard and watched as a ghostly hand materialized, pointing to the ceiling in the corner of the living room. Grabbing a chair and turning on the light, I carried it to the corner where it was pointing.

"Who are you?" I asked. I watched as the ghostly body flickered the shape of a woman and disappeared. "Okay, I didn't quite catch that, but what am I looking for?" No answer. I guess that was all I was getting for tonight. Checking thoroughly the corner where the spirit was pointing, I found a small hook. When I pulled it out, a click sounded in the floor below me. I put the chair back to where I got it. After making sure Raylene and Adam were still asleep, I went to check the floor. At the base of the baseboard, a section had come loose. I pulled it off and stuck my fingers inside. A small thin box was at the back. I carefully pulled it out and replaced the baseboard. I heard a sound from upstairs and quickly sat on the couch, sliding the box under my butt. I picked up the journal and pretended to be reading it.

"Emily, you're up late. Are you okay?" Raylene asked.

"Yeah, I guess I just needed to read it again, to know."

"Know what?"

"What's going to happen to me."

"Emily, we've been through this," she said, looking to the corner of the living room I had just left.

"I know, but I wouldn't blame you if you did it. Dad wanted you to. I am just glad I get to be prepared."

Raylene came down to sit beside me.

"I know he told me, but it wouldn't feel right. I will still check out the other families though, just to see if it is possible for both of us, okay?" I nodded. I couldn't help but think that she didn't seem to have any issues with it when I didn't know about it. "I know you are having issues trusting me, and I don't blame you at all. But I have to ask, were you in the room when Ben died?"

"We all were. Why?"

"I mean, the whole time?"

"I don't understand the question, Ray. What are you getting at?"

"Okay, I am only going to ask this once, but how sure are you that Adam didn't kill James and Ben?"

"What? Ray, how can you even think that?"

"Just listen for a minute please." I kept silent. "When James died, Adam was upstairs doing the window with Ben, he was on the roof. And it just so happens that the glass falls, killing your boyfriend?"

"We had broken up; he was not my boyfriend. There would have been no reason to."

"A technicality he was coming to talk to you to try and get you back, wasn't he? Anyway, then my fiancé ends up dead not too long after. So, both of us end up single and then he is dating you, but asks me to marry him? To me, it seems like he is trying to cover all his bases."

"Adam is not like that, Ray. He is sweet and kind, and has only tried to help through all of this."

"Yes, coincidentally a very attractive boy from our childhood that we grew up with is single and willing to help with whatever we need help with."

"Ray, you know why he is single."

"Yes, but that he is just that nice to put his life on hold to help us out of our situation."

"Ray, stop. Not everyone has an ulterior motive," I said, looking at her sternly.

"Are you saying I do?"

"Don't you? You slept with James to break us up, now you are going after Adam."

"No, he asked me."

"You expect me to believe you over him?"

"Yes, I am your sister."

"Who has been lying to me since we were kids, who would have let me die if not for your fiancé's death? Which, by the way, you could have helped to his death. How do I know you had nothing to do with it? You were in the room the longest."

"What? Emily, how could you think I had anything to do with—?"

"The same way you can accuse Adam, who has done nothing but help me so much to get through this."

"Why would I want him dead? Give me one possible reason."

"Simple, he backed out of wanting to marry you to save my life. That hurt you. By killing him, you got your revenge and opened up the option to take Adam from me, who already knew about everything going on and might be easy to convince to marry you." She looked at me, horrified that I would suggest such a thing.

"Fine, forget I said anything. I told you I would only say it once. I was just thinking about it and it was just a thought. Their deaths so close to each other and all."

"Well, good, never bring it up again." I was furious at her that she could accuse Adam. Just as I saw she was furious that I accused her, I pretended to read the journal, hoping she would go away. I kept looking at her eyeing the top corner of the living room where I pulled the hook. More and more I kept thinking that she had seen or heard the spirits too. I was debating asking her when she stood up, she said she was tired, and went back to bed.

I grabbed the box that I was sitting on, and making sure I waited till I heard her door close, I opened it. There was a brass key with a gold ribbon tied to the top. It was old. Wound around the middle of the key was a piece of paper. The rest of the box was covered in red velvet. Nothing else was in it.

A creek at the top of the stairwell made me panic. I dropped the key down my shirt and stared at the empty box. Another creek made me turn my head.

Raylene slowly walked down the stairs. She took a step, waited three seconds, and took another step.

"Ray, are you okay?" She didn't answer. She continued down; take a step, pause, take a step, pause. "Are you awake?" I asked, slowly approaching her. That was a stupid question. It was not like she could answer if she was sleeping.

I didn't know what to do, you are not supposed to wake sleepwalkers, are you?

"Adam," I called. She got to the bottom of the stairs and smiled as she turned to me.

"How are you, Emily?" she said softly. "Are you sleeping well?"

"Yes, fine, thank you," I replied, playing along. "Adam," I called again, growing more concerned.

"You shouldn't yell so, Emily," she said, smiling. She almost did a pirouette, as she turned to walk out of the room, heading to the kitchen. I considered running to get Adam, but didn't want to leave Raylene alone; Ben almost drowned when he was sleepwalking. She was acting funny, and the last people that were not acting like themselves are both dead. I called one more time for Adam before following Raylene to the kitchen. She was acting like she was preparing an imaginary cup of tea.

"We need to do this more often; we don't talk anymore."

"What do you want to talk about?"

"You, of course. So how are the plans going for the big day, Emily? Adam—" she squealed, as he entered the room.

"She has the names right, but everything else is not her," I quickly explained to him. "Adam, do you think if we all left and didn't come back...Do you think this could all stop?"

"No," Raylene yelled, "you belong here, you can't leave." Her sweet calm demeanor changed. She lunged at me, grabbing at my hair as I tried to get away. "You are all mine. You gave yourself to me."

"Okay, we won't go," I said. She released my hair and went back to making her pretend tea. So much for that idea. Adam looked at me, relieved that the situation was diffused. He was probably not too keen on the idea of attacking Raylene.

"So, what now?" he asked.

"I want to hear all about your wedding plans. Don't leave anything out."

"Wedding plans?" he asked, looking at me.

"I spent so much time getting the two of you together, of course there is going to be a wedding." Adam looked at me, confused. My head started to ache. Two minutes later, I was on the floor, trying to hold back the tears.

"Emily, are you okay?" Raylene said, running up to me. The pain subsided and Raylene was Raylene again. She, of course, didn't remember a thing, and was wondering what she was doing in the kitchen. We explained what happened and she freaked out. She started pacing around the kitchen, biting her nails. She looked nervous. I had never seen her like this before.

"What's wrong? Do you know something we don't?" I asked calmly, hoping she wouldn't get upset with me for asking.

"Ben and James were acting weird and they are gone. Am I going to be next?" She stared at me, tears welling in her eyes.

"Well, then, we can go together. Strange things have been happening to me as well."

"Like what?"

"Hearing and seeing things that aren't there."

"Oh." She looked uncomfortable when I said that, but brushed it off quickly. After she left the room and went back to bed, Adam and I went back to my bedroom. I showed the key to Adam that I had found earlier that night.

"What is it for?" he asked. I shrugged.

"There was a piece of paper around it."

"It's not here now," he said. We went back downstairs, retracing my steps, checking under everything. We didn't find it.

"Do you think Ray might have found it?" I asked.

"I don't know, we were kind of preoccupied."

"Yeah, maybe tomorrow in the light, we will have better luck."

"Yeah," he said, sounding disappointed.

"What's wrong?" I asked, when we were back in bed.

"Nothing."

"That's not true."

"Fine. But don't laugh."

"Okay."

"I was just thinking that it would be disappointing if this ended like this. A mysterious key with no door to open. A lost note that wasn't read. How often do adults find a treasure hunt that was laid out with secret panels and latches? Hidden drawers. All being led by a mysterious spirit, right in their own home."

"Well, when you put it that way, yes, it would be a shame for it to end this way. But I don't think it is the end. The spirit isn't done yet. Because I haven't found what she wants me to find yet."

"Did you actually get to see her?"

"Only a flicker, but the image was a woman."

"A woman? Did you recognize her?"

"No," I said, shaking my head.

"I wonder who would have something that important to say."

"Who knows, maybe everyone gets told to do this."

"And they put everything back in the exact same spot? Every generation?"

"Hmm, well, maybe not."

By the time I woke up, it was afternoon. I found Raylene and Adam in the kitchen.

"How are you feeling?" Raylene asked.

"Fine. I slept really well." They looked at each other then back at me.

"You don't remember?" Adam asked.

"Obviously not," I said, annoyed.

They proceeded to tell me that I was sleepwalking last night. I had walked to Dad's grave, sat down, looked like I was having a conversation with him, and went for a walk around the property. It was morning before I finally decided to come back in.

"We were worried you would do it again, so we stayed up."

"You didn't have to do that. I am sure I would have been fine." I was concerned that I didn't remember it. I remembered my other conversations with Dad. I somehow didn't believe what they were telling me was real. But something was off. Up till now, this all seemed to be directed at me. James attacking me, Ben sleepwalking, telling me I belonged with him, Raylene telling me I couldn't leave because she had worked so hard to get Adam and me together. Obviously, someone or something in this house was working overtime to get us together, to keep us here. So, why all of a sudden would I be the one sleepwalking and not remembering, there was no purpose to it. But then, if it wasn't real, why would they both be lying about it. I looked from Adam to Raylene. Unless…

"So, I guess it would be my turn next," Adam said, snapping me out of my thoughts.

"For what?" Raylene asked.

"To be possessed. Both of you have, I don't want to be left out," he said, laughing.

"Possessed? That is stupid," I said.

"Really, Adam, that is not funny."

"It was just weird sleepwalking that we have never done before," I said.

"Yeah," Raylene said. "Why on earth would you think it was possession?"

"I guess I misspoke," he said. He knew we did not like that word. Although thinking about it, he might not be wrong. We knew that there was a spirit helping me with all these clues to find out something that it wanted me to know. Was that too much of a stretch to think it could use our bodies while we were sleeping? The thought terrified me. So far it hasn't done anything to hurt Raylene and me, but how could we be sure it wouldn't?

"Adam, please don't mention it again," I said. I took a cup of coffee out on the porch. It looked like it might rain again today. This was not normal weather for this time of year. We have not had this much rain since I was a kid. The year I built the music box. I couldn't help but wonder if the music box Adam gave back to me the day before Raylene arrived might have saved me in some way. Even if we weren't officially engaged, it was an item we both made together. And Dad said it had us both. Yet, someone was helping me. I should leave. I had a small place in the city still, Raylene and Adam could do whatever they wanted, if they wanted to be together, I wouldn't be in the way. And if…if I had to die, so be it.

"You can't go; I won't let you," I heard a voice say. The voice sounded male, harsh, almost like I was being scolded for even thinking it. Did it really know what I was thinking or was it guessing, since I was staring at my car?

"Why?"

"I chose you; I want you."

"For what?"

"You are mine."

"No, Ray was chosen." Great, I was arguing with someone I couldn't see.

"You will not go." He seemed to be getting louder and madder.

"Who are you?" There was no answer. "Why did you choose me?"

"I want you," his voice getting more intense.

"Emily…" Adam called, peering his head out the door. Spotting me, he came and sat beside me. "Talking to yourself?" I looked at him and shook my head. "She is back?" I shook my head again. He looked shocked, but didn't push the issue.

After calling out for him a couple of times and getting no reply, I figured he was gone, and that it was safe enough to talk to Adam. I told him my fears of what it would mean for Raylene if the voice got his way. Adam seemed upset, but relieved. Understandable, I guess, in his situation, it would be a good thing. A shadow moved at the window behind us. Had she heard? Did she hear all of it?

"So much for our deal," Raylene said, after I went back inside.

"What are you talking about?"

"I heard what you said."

"And what did you hear exactly? That the spirit is telling me I can't leave. I wanted to go home, and it told me I can't."

"But…You…"

"You heard what you wanted to hear. I was going to go home and let you do what you needed to do, it said no. I don't think it is going to let any of us leave. If the spirit is keeping me here, yes, I am worried, and talking with Adam is helping to keep me sane. Especially, since only one of us is supposed to survive this mess. Any other conclusions you want to jump to?" I asked her, annoyed. She looked shocked. Looking away sheepishly, she shook her head.

I saw Adam watching us from the outside of the room. His eyes fixated on Raylene. Was he considering saving himself by actually marrying Raylene? He caught me looking at him and made himself scarce. It was getting harder and harder to understand his facial features. Had Raylene gotten into my head, blaming him for the deaths? Was I starting to think he might have been able to…? No, that was not possible, he has never shown any signs of aggression. And why? None of this was making any sense and it was driving me crazy to think that Adam could have anything to do with this. Although, if he did, would that make Raylene next on his list? He already knew I would never be able to do it. Or would it be me? Could he and Raylene have a plan to kill me? Although, they could do that just by getting married.

My head was starting to hurt, and I can go around and round with these ideas and conspiracies. It wouldn't do any good. I had to pay more attention; I had to find out what was going on. Raylene had already seduced James, it wouldn't be farfetched to think she would be able to do it again.

"Emily?" Raylene called.

"Yeah."

"Where were you? I have been calling your name for the last two minutes."

"I've been here; I haven't moved."

"Physically, maybe, but mentally, you were not here."

"Just thinking."

"Obviously, about what?"

"Silly stuff. Crazy stuff. Doesn't matter. So, any plans for today?" I said, quickly trying to change the topic.

"I was going to take a walk."

"It is nice right now, but looks like it will rain later." This small talk was getting awkward and Raylene felt it too. I tapped my fingers on the table a couple of times, trying to think of something to say. Raylene noticed.

Not wanting to make things more awkward, I left and decided to do some cleaning. By the time I got back to the kitchen, Raylene was gone. I happened to glance out the window and caught sight of Adam talking with Raylene by the tree line. She kept moving closer to him, was she going to slap him or kiss him? A few seconds later, it was him that moved in to kiss her and within a few more seconds, their arms were wrapped around each other.

Chapter 11

I had had enough. They could have each other. With tears streaming down my face, I went up to my room to pack. With a bag over my shoulder, I went back downstairs.

"No," I heard a voice yell behind me.

"Yes," I yelled back, "you can have Ray and Adam. You don't need me. I can wait for my death in the city."

"I said NO," the voice yelled again. I almost didn't realize that it happened and maybe I imagined it, but I could swear that I saw one of the wood panels behind me from the wall move and my bag flew across the room and hit the wall, the zipper broke and spilled the contents onto the floor. I turned around, but the wood was back in place, as if it had never moved. But if I imagined it, how did my bag get knocked across the room? I looked over at my bag. The antique brass key fell out of the front pocket of the bag and I walked over to it and picked it up. The note. Looking out the window, I made sure they were not walking to the house; they were nowhere to be seen. I went to the kitchen and started looking for the note. It had been squished into a crack between the floor and the baseboard.

I grabbed a fork and stuck one of the tines in the hole of the rolled paper, carefully pulling it out. Hearing noises on the porch, I quickly hid the note down my shirt and started wiping down the counters. A short time later, Adam was watching me from the kitchen doorway.

"Did you have a good walk?" I asked, looking at him.

"You saw?"

I nodded. "You are looking out for yourself. I get it."

"Emily, I—"

"Stop, please. Just…don't…I don't want to be used. I don't want to die, but I have more self-respect than letting this happen all over again. I did that once. Both you and Raylene told me I deserved better. So why would I accept it willingly when you do it?" I was furious.

"I—"

"Look, I don't care that you are with her, you can marry her tomorrow, for all I care. I just would like to know why I can't leave. I tried to leave, and my bag got thrown across the room. If you can control the spirits, tell them to let me go so I can die in peace."

"Emily, you're bleeding," Adam said, looking at me, shocked. The fork I was holding in my hand and had been pushing into the counter to hold in my anger, I had actually been pushing into my arm.

I looked down, shocked, blood seeped out of my skin. There was no pain. I removed the fork from my arm and watched the blood ooze out of the wound.

Adam looked scared. I ran my arm under cold water and wrapped it with paper towel. He and I both knew. I was probably going to start having more accidents again.

"You know what. I won't go, you guys can watch all the accidents and deteriorating health that I have to go through. Why should I die alone, when I can make you guys watch everything? Just tell me why?"

"Emily, I am doing this for us. To get information from her."

"What?"

"If she thinks I'm with you, she won't tell us anything. If she thinks I am leaning her way, we have more of a chance to get information. We already know she has no issues seducing your boyfriends." I was skeptical. Why would we need information from her, we all knew what was going on. I didn't know whether to believe him or not. For now, I decided not to show him the note.

"Adam, I don't know about this. I just went through this with James, I don't think I can overlook it anymore."

"Emily, please. I am doing this for us," he said, coming up to me and wrapping his arms around me. "I could never care for your sister the way I do for you. I also will be looking into helping your sister find someone from one of the other families to marry into while I am getting information from her."

"Fine, just try to make sure I don't see you. Actually, seeing it is worse than knowing it is happening."

"Yes, ma'am. Now let's get you bandaged up," he said, kissing my forehead. I nodded.

"I guess this is a bonus."

"What?" he asked, grabbing a Band-Aid from the bathroom.

"Me injuring myself again will make it look like you are sincere," I said, walking over to my bag and cleaning up the clothes.

"Why did you do it?"

"I didn't know I did. I thought it was the counter." He looked at me, concerned. "I need to go lay down." He grabbed my bag for me when it was cleaned up and helped me up the stairs.

There was something he wasn't telling me, I thought, as I laid down and waited for him to leave the room. After he left, I pushed the thoughts of Raylene and Adam out of my mind. I pulled the note out of my bra and carefully rolled it open. It was written in a solid, black fountain pen, almost calligraphy writing. No one writes that way anymore, it kind of brought a smile to my face to see such an elaborate plan that someone put into place that revealed fancy writing and all.

If you have found this, it means that everything I have planned and tried to put in place to warn you has finally worked. Please keep going, find the door that this key opens, there will be more waiting when you do.

I hid the note under the mattress. For now, I wouldn't tell Adam anything. I looked out the window and saw Adam storming out of the house, charging off in the same direction of where he and Raylene were kissing; he looked mad. Was he mad that I caught him?

Not knowing how long I had, I started downstairs. Thinking the key probably opened a basement or extra room, I knew that upstairs, there wasn't room for something like that to be hidden. After all we had done, the secret drawer, and the hidden compartment in the wall, was it such a stretch to think there could be a hidden room as well? I scoured every wall for a hidden keyhole, moved almost every can in the pantry. I checked the floors; maybe there was a trapdoor somewhere.

I was about to start checking the living room when I heard arguing on the front porch. Should I listen or bolt upstairs? I was about to make the decision to go upstairs, when I heard:

"We could do it tonight, she won't know," Raylene said. I couldn't hear Adam's response, but I assumed he said no.

"Why? She wouldn't know till it was going to start hurting her again," Raylene said.

"It's not right to go behind her back, we should at least tell her face to face."

"That will just make it harder."

"And how do you think she will react when she learns you lied to her again?"

"At some point, it would have to be done, and she knows it. It will be easier on her if it was done after."

"You mean, it would be easier on you," I said, opening the door. Both looked at me shocked.

"Emily."

"Don't...Please don't try to cover it up. I know what I heard, and I understand. But I am not going to accept a half-assed project in exchange for my life. Give me one week. I want to be alone, accident-free for one week. So, you both leave, build something worthy of my life, and I won't stand in your way."

Neither of them knew what to say, they stared at me blankly.

"Are you sure that is what you want?" Adam asked.

"No, but it is what is going to happen. My sister was the one chosen by my dad. And I messed it up by learning about it. I am not okay with any of it, how could anyone be? Although, it seems that Ray decided the best way to do this was to go after you instead of checking the other families like she said she was going to do," I said, glaring at her. Again, they didn't say anything for a long time.

"But what about the blackouts, what if that happens and we aren't here?" Adam asked.

"So far, they have been harmless, and if they decide to kill me, at least you guys don't have to worry about it later."

They looked at each other again. Adam's face looked guilty. It was me he was playing. I should have known. He knew I would never agree to the ritual knowing it would kill Raylene. So, he chose her. I couldn't blame him, really. Having a choice to live or die, I guess the choice is simple.

"So, you guys gonna leave or what?"

"Umm...yeah," Raylene said.

"One week." I stated again.

"Sure." They both nodded.

"And I expect something amazing when you come back."

"Okay." They both went upstairs to pack. I stayed out of their way till they were about to leave. I gave them each a hug, told them to bring lots of alcohol and first-aid supplies; if I was going to have a bunch of injuries, they would be a necessity. They laughed a little with me, but felt awkward about it. A short time later, I waved to them driving down the road. I turned on every single light in the house.

"Okay, house, you are not going to beat me. You want me for some reason. Well, I am not giving up. Someone wants to help me, now I just need to figure out why. Where is the hidden door?" I said. "We have one week to figure out what you want me to know," I said, now talking to the spirit instead of the house. I searched every corner upstairs and down. I moved every piece of furniture; it was late into the next day when I finally found it. It was a simple crack in the floorboard. It had been there forever. I moved the chair further away and stuck the key into the floor till it wouldn't move anymore. Slowly, turned the key till it clicked. Okay, now to find a handle. Nope, none. I grabbed the fireplace poker. Not seeing a clear edge, I tried pulling the key, seeing if any of the floor lifted. As soon as I saw the edge, I stuck the poker in and opened the trapdoor. A spider crawled up my arm. I screamed and dropped the door. Cobwebs and dust flew everywhere. I grabbed the fireplace shovel and smashed it on the spider who scurried to find a new hiding place. I again tried to hit him and he crawled into the corner under the baseboard.

"Any more of you guys down there?" I laughed at how freaked out the spider was making me when I was dealing with spirits and voices just fine. Or maybe I wasn't dealing with any of this, maybe I was just pushing it out of my mind because I was dealing with other stuff with James and Ben and now Raylene and Adam.

After making sure the spider wasn't going to come out of hiding, I stuck the poker back in the corner and pulled it up. I flipped it over, strings of thick, dust-covered webs came with it. No more movement. A disgusting smell came from below. I rummaged around till I found the flashlight that got thrown to the corner of the room when the spider crawled on me. I slowly descended the stairs. No one had been down here for a very long time; layers of dust covered every inch of the steps and the floor. I found a small light hanging above me at the bottom of the stairs. I pulled on the chain; it didn't turn on. No surprise. Why would a light work in a creepy, dark, hidden basement? I slowly moved the light around the edge of the room. A desk, covered in dust, a toilet, a bed. As I moved closer to the bed, I noticed the body. I guess, not actually a body. Bones. Positioned as if whoever it was just fell asleep and never woke up. I wanted to run. But someone wanted me to find this place and certainly not just for the bones. Taking a deep breath and calming my nerves, I scanned the room again and walked over to the desk. Laying right in the middle was another journal, dust covered it. I wiped it off. It was the same. It was like the one that was buried in my mother's grave. This must be it. This was what the spirit wanted me to find. I grabbed it and ran back up the stairs; cleaning could wait. I had to know. I went straight for my bedroom and began reading.

My name is Maggie. I don't have much time left, and I hope one day someone will find this and end this once and for all.

The cabin kills. I have seen it, so many that I loved have died here. The ritual triggers it. You activate the curse. They all think it is a blessing, but it is not, everyone dies. Even my brother. It was me who was supposed to do the ritual. My brother found out and did it before I got the chance. Once he saw what it was doing to me, he and his wife locked me down here. They couldn't stand to see what was happening to me.

105

I lost track of time. I am very weak. I don't think I will last much longer. I hope they never have children. I hope this curse dies with them. I don't blame my brother for what he did. After all, I was going to do it too. It seems like this ritual wasn't for us, it wasn't to help us, it might have been at one point, but not anymore. I think once the cabin has you, it decides. I might be crazy, right? Maybe I wasn't thinking clearly anymore. No, wait, that is wrong, something. There is more. I don't have the time to figure this all out. I don't have the time to make sense of any of this. I am trapped down here; I can't do anything.

It is too late for me. Too late for my brother and his wife. I am hoping this ends here, but if they have children, I hope I can help them. I hope I can warn them. I won't be alive. I would have been dead long before they were born. But hopefully they can find this, hopefully someone has the sense to stop this insanity. It is tearing our families apart for nothing because we don't get to finish living our lives. The ritual starts tearing everything apart as soon as someone gets told about the ritual.

By the last few lines, I could see Maggie struggling to get the words written. I would have to show Raylene. But not now. I would do it tomorrow. For now, I needed to sleep. I tucked the journal under the pillow and closed my eyes.

When I woke up, nothing was where I had left it. I was wearing different clothes. The journal was moved, it was not under the pillow. I made my way downstairs. Everything was back where it was supposed to be; the trapdoor was closed. The dust was all cleaned up.

"Adam, what is going on? You are not supposed to be here," I said groggily.

"You called Raylene over yesterday. I hadn't heard from her, so I came over. Where is she, Emily?"

"I don't know. I have been sleeping. I was going to call her when I woke up, but that was today."

"She said you called. That you needed to talk to her right away."

"Yes, I do need to talk to her. I found something, but I was so tired I didn't get a chance to talk to her. I fell asleep. I found another journal, from a woman named Maggie."

"You mean this one?" he said, holding up the journal.

"Yes. I wanted to show it to Ray, see if she believed it."

"Where is she, Emily?"

"I don't know. Like I said, I just woke up. Wait, why are you accusing me and exactly what do you think I did?"

"She came here to see you; her car is in the driveway. Where is she?" Adam started raising his voice, he was starting to scare me.

"I don't know, I haven't seen her, I swear it." Tears started welling in my eyes, as he continued to yell at me, assuming I had anything to do with her disappearing.

"Emily, please, if you have done anything to her, it is okay, just tell me where she is."

"Adam, I really don't know." I started crying. "I was the one who said I wouldn't go through with this. You two were. The two of you were going to kill me, remember?"

"Maybe we were, but it looks like you have taken care of that."

"No," I yelled. "I wouldn't do anything to hurt her." I was getting mad now. I was getting tired of his accusations.

"Emily."

"No, don't say another word. Get out."

"Not till you tell me where she is."

"I don't know," I said, screaming. "Get out." And with all the force I could muster, I shoved him to the door. He grabbed me, and I squirmed to get free, but he held me too tight. I stomped hard on his foot; his grip loosened slightly. I squirmed again in his arms. I got an elbow free and elbowed him in the gut. Finally getting him to let me go, I ran to my room and locked the door.

"Just tell me where she is, Emily, I will leave you alone after."

"I haven't seen her. The last time I saw her, you were driving off together." The door vibrated as he punched it. I heard him swearing on the other side. I listened as he walked away. I curled up in bed and pulled the blankets tight around me.

"You can wake up now," I heard a voice say in my dream.

My eyes fluttered awake. I felt tired and sore. I had bruises on my arms and waist from earlier. I looked out the window. Adam's and Raylene's cars were still outside. I listened at the door; I heard no sounds.

I didn't know what mood either would be in, but I couldn't stay in here much longer. I was hungry and thirsty, and really had to go to the washroom. I unlocked the door and held my breath as I slowly opened it. Everything seemed eerily calm. I ran my hand along the wall, as I made my way downstairs. Still no sign of Raylene and Adam. I came out of the washroom and went to make something to eat.

Did I dream it all? I almost would have believed that if not for the bruises. I ate my sandwich, as the water started to boil in the kettle. The familiar whistling was soothing. I added the water to my awaiting cup.

I went to sit on the porch, as I blew the tea to cool it down. When I looked into the cup, it was no longer tea. It was blood. I dropped the cup and watched as the mug shattered and the blood seeped into the cracks of the porch. The blood started to spread and cover the whole porch. Looking over the steps, I saw James's body. It stood up. With the chunk of glass still in his head, he started reaching for me.

"Wake up," I heard a voice say.

I snapped my eyes open; it was just a dream. My heart was beating fast. Looking around, I was still in my bed. I didn't want to leave the room, but I really did need to use the washroom, and eat and get a drink. I looked out the window, Adam's and Raylene's cars were out there.

I opened the door, no one was there. Making sure not to mimic my dream, I kept my hand away from the wall. Should I call out to see if Adam and Raylene were there? I went to the washroom, brewed coffee instead of tea. I did not go outside. Not that I expected my coffee to turn into blood or anything. That would be crazy.

I cleaned up and took a walk around back to Dad's grave. I sat staring at his headstone.

"Dad, I wish you were here. I need answers. I don't know what is happening. I don't know how any of you could have done any of this. The person I thought you were, the people you told me about, our family. I don't understand."

I don't know what I was expecting, but I got no answers. I stayed out there for a couple of hours before I gave up. Walking back to the front of the house, both vehicles were still there. I was a little nervous going into the house and calling their names, but I was starting to get concerned.

I checked every room, didn't find either of them. I checked the lake; the boat was still tied to the dock. I walked into the woods in the direction I watched them walk earlier this week. Not that I wanted to find them there if they were there; I have a pretty good idea what they were doing there. Nope, didn't find them. I was running out of options of where to look for them.

As I was approaching the cabin on my way back, I saw a dark shadow moving inside the house. I quickened my pace, maybe the spirit had some answers for me.

As I entered, the ghostly image stopped and turned toward me. It was not the woman that had been helping me before, this one was male. This one was very angry; was it angry at me? Did I not do something he wanted me to? The intensity of the way he stared at me scared me. I didn't know whether to scream and run or talk to him. James's words suddenly echoed in my head.

"He wants you." Could this be the 'he' that he had been talking about? I had already figured out it wasn't Adam, even though it pointed to him at the time. I thought he was crazy because I knew Adam was not like that. Maybe he knew, maybe he knew all along about this one. Not the spirits, they were here to help me. And if James didn't mean the spirit, maybe he meant the house. The cabin already admitted that it wanted me, that it wouldn't let me go. Could this be the spirit of the cabin? I walked toward the living room. The spirit matched my movements. He kept staring.

"Are you here to—" I couldn't finish my sentence. He charged at me and I fell backwards. When I woke up, I was in my bed. How did I get here? Maybe Adam or Raylene found me? I left my room and started calling for them.

There was no reply. Looking out the window, their vehicles were still outside. After checking the whole cabin, I started to panic. Was Adam right? Did I do something to them?

Then I remembered the basement. No, no, no. I wouldn't. I couldn't. I rushed to try and lift the trapdoor. My fingers fumbled and dropped it. I scrambled to get a good hold and lifted it up. Quickly, I ran down the steps. I crumpled to the ground, clutching my stomach. Raylene was bound and gagged to the chair by the desk. The chair was overturned.

"Ray?" I whispered when I could finally speak. I slowly crawled over to her. I knew she was dead, but I couldn't stop myself, I had to see. I pulled on the edge of the chair till the chair tipped toward me.

I looked at Raylene in horror as I saw the wound on her neck. Someone had slit her throat, there was so much blood, and she was covered in it. Her wrists were sheered almost to the bone, probably from trying to get free. I couldn't breathe. With tears streaming down my face and gasping for breath, I ran upstairs and outside. I ran till my legs collapsed under me. I screamed. I curled up on the ground gasping for breath.

Did I do this to her? No, it couldn't have been. I hadn't seen her. Adam? But he's been missing too.

"Emily," Adam's panicked voice came running through my head.

"Emily." Adam's arms grabbed me off the ground. He slid my arms around his neck and put his around my waist and knees. He carried me back to the cabin.

"Did I? Did you? What happened to her, Adam?" I choked out; I felt numb. How could I have done something like that to her?

"Shhh, we'll discuss it later. Right now, rest, I'll get you some tea," he said, after putting me down on the couch. I pulled my knees up to my chest and rocked back and forth. How could she be dead? The images of her refused to leave my mind.

"Emily?" Adam said. I looked up at him and grabbed the tea he was holding in front of me.

"Was it you?" I looked at him blankly. I couldn't believe either of us could do something like that, but I was obviously wrong. One of us did. He turned away from my gaze.

"I—"

"If you are going to tell me you did it for me, you can stop right there," I said coldly.

"I couldn't let her do what she was planning to do."

"And what was that? You were both going to be able to live through this."

"I..." He turned to look at me. "I wanted you from the beginning, you should have known that. It was always you."

"And that is supposed to make this go away? You killed my sister, Adam. How am I supposed to live with that?" A look of pain spread across his face.

"I knew you would never do it, and I couldn't let you die," he said, getting angry.

"You have no right to be angry with me about this, Adam."

"I know, you're right, I'm sorry."

"Sorry, seriously, Adam. I can't deal with this right now."

"Look, what is done is done, just tell me what you want, and I'll do it. We don't have to worry about any of the other stuff anymore."

"Right now, I am going to my room. You are going to bury my sister out back with my parents." I put my tea down and left him standing there. He tried calling out for me to stop, but I didn't listen. Late into the night, I heard him digging and dragging her body out from the basement. I cried silently that night.

Later, I felt Adam staring at me from that doorway and turned to face him.

"Why would you do it? You could have been married to her and gone through with the ritual. That is what you wanted."

"No," he said, dropping to his knees beside the bed, grabbing my hand. "It is not what I wanted. I wanted you. It has always been you. Why do you think I gave you that music box back, it was our addition to the house. Yours and mine. It has always been you." He brought my hand to his lips and kissed it.

"Adam, how do you expect me to live my life knowing you killed her?"

"I don't know," he said, turning away. "I guess I was hoping you would love me enough to understand why I did what I did."

"I know why you did it," I said, sitting up. "I just don't know if I can forgive it." He nodded. He got up, but did not let go of my hand.

"I guess I should go."

"Adam, this must have been hard for you to do. And even though I can't agree with what you've done. Thank you. I may not know what comes next, but I now have a bit of time to figure things out." He nodded and turned to leave. "Adam...please...stay."

"Are you sure?" he said, coming back to my side, looking hopeful.

"You are the only one left. Everyone else is gone. And I don't want to be alone. So, if you don't mind—"

"Of course, I don't mind. Whatever you need, I am here for you." He sat on the bed with his back in the headboard, and I curled up beside him with my head on his chest. He wrapped his arms around me. I told him about the blackouts I have been having. There was no one else I could talk to about any of this. I knew deep down he would help me through this no matter how I treated him. And as much as I wanted to hate him for what he did to Raylene, I couldn't. How many people can say their partners would kill for them? Adam showed me he would, no matter who it was. He risked me hating him forever just to save my life.

Adam was not around for the next few days; his dad had a lot of work for him to do at the store. I guess that it was good not having him around; I was not feeling well, was dizzy and nauseous. Adam thought it was probably dealing with Raylene's death that was causing me to feel sick. But I wasn't so sure.

"Emily, wake up," Adam's panicked voice stirred me out of my sleep. I was numb. I couldn't feel my body.

"What's going on?" I asked groggily.

"What the hell are you doing?" he shouted.

"Sleeping?" I said, confused. "What else would I have been doing?"

"In your mother's grave? Are you trying to tell me something?"

"What?" I asked looking around, suddenly aware of my surroundings. "How did I get out here?"

"Wait, you don't remember coming out here?" I shook my head. Adam helped me out of the grave. I was covered in dirt from head to toe. It seemed I dug the grave with my bare hands.

Adam wrapped my arms around his neck and lifted me up to carry me into the house. After making me a cup of tea, he started a fire, then went to run me a bath.

"Come on, let's get you cleaned up." I allowed him to drag me along and later, he tucked me into bed.

"Thank you."

"Should I be worried?" he asked.

"What do you mean?"

"I mean, the black outs, the sleepwalking, whatever you want to call it?"

"Honestly, I don't know, but so far, nothing bad has happened that I know of, and I haven't been hurt."

"Maybe we should talk to someone, see if it is normal?"

"Will anyone answer even if they knew? We could ask your mom, but if she doesn't know, I doubt the others will risk it."

"I will ask her. In the meantime, if you want something to help you sleep. Might help with the sleepwalking?"

"No, it should be okay." He did not look reassured, but nodded and left, closing the door behind him. I felt physically exhausted, but my mind was racing. Did I really dig that grave with my hands? And why? Was one of the spirits trying to tell me something again?

It was some time before I finally decided it was pointless to try and sleep. I was about to head downstairs when I heard Adam talking to someone.

"I don't know if I can get her to go through with it," Adam said.

"Is she that bad?" the other man said. He sounded familiar. I just couldn't remember, maybe I was too tired to think clearly.

"Yeah, things are happening too quickly and she is not handling it well. I think it is just too much at once. And then there is the other stuff."

"What stuff?"

"I...They have interfered before but never to this extent. It is different. She is different."

"Do you think it is because she knows too much? That other journal kind of popped up out of nowhere. We need to get rid of it before it spreads to the rest of them."

"Yeah..."

"You okay?" I finally recognized the voice as belonging to Rick.

"This was not supposed to get this messed up."

"Everyone is gone now that could have messed this up for you. You just have to finish it."

"I know, I know," Adam sounded unconvinced.

"Look, Adam, you said she was willing to die to let you and her sister live. All that has changed is that her sister is dead, so why wouldn't she still want you to live?"

"Because she THINKS I killed her sister."

"Wait...You haven't told her the truth?"

"How am I supposed to do that with how she is feeling? Yeah, Emily, just so you know, you got possessed and killed your sister." I gasped, they heard me.

"Emily, I..." Adam said when he saw me.

With tears welling up in my eyes, I turned and ran back into my room and locked the door.

Did I really do it? Adam would have no reason to lie, would he? And if I did this to Raylene, what about the others, could I have done those too? I couldn't stop the tears, they rolled down my cheeks and onto my knees that I had pulled up to my chest and was hugging tightly. Adam was knocking lightly at the door, calling my name.

"I'm so sorry, Emily, please let me in—"

"Leave me alone. I can't—"

"We don't have to talk; I can just hold you…be with you…you don't have to be alone."

"Adam, just go." I heard him sigh on the other side of the door. He stopped knocking and I heard him slide down the door. He was going to sit there for me?

"I will wait as long as you need," he said softly. A while later, I heard him leave and return. "There is a tray of food out here if you're hungry." I could hear a hint of pleading in his voice, he was worried about me. I wiped the tears from my eyes and took a few deep breaths. Slowly rising from the bed, I headed to the door and unlocked it, returning to the bed and laid down with my back toward the door. I heard the door open; Adam slowly entered the room and placed the tray of food at the end of the bed. I scooted over a bit and Adam came to sit beside me. He slowly laid down next to me and draped an arm around my waist, pressing his chest against my back.

He was warm and comforting, and somehow knew not to talk. I rolled over and buried my face into his chest. He gently rubbed my back and kissed the top of my head. I didn't know how long I laid in his arms, but by the time I unwrapped myself from him, he was fast asleep. As carefully as I could, I climbed out of bed and left the room. I pulled the door close as quietly as I could. I placed my hand on the door and took a deep breath. *I can do this,* I thought to myself. I headed downstairs to the kitchen. I made a small grocery list, grabbed my purse and the car keys.

"Where are you going?" Adam asked from the top of the stairs.

"To town, I was going to make us a special dinner tonight as a surprise, which you kind of now spoiled," I said, smirking.

"Let me drive you," Adam said, as he made his way down the stairs.

"Really, you don't have to. I will be back in about an hour. You have been so good to take care of me lately with everything going on, and I really want to do this for you."

"Are you okay to drive?" I walked up to him at the foot of the stairs and kissed him.

"I am more than okay. I will be back soon." I kissed him again and turned to leave.

"I'll be waiting," he said. I turned back to him and gave him a slight smile.

"Dinner will be worth it, I promise."

"Can't wait." I hopped in my car and drove into town, half not believing I got away with it. I was expecting him to be more forceful in stopping me. The other half, terrified. I drove into the market parking-lot. Breathing as normally as I could, I got out. As I approached the store, I noticed a lot of eyes watching me. Not all, just…just the ones from the families. Did Adam call them? Did he ask them to watch me? My heart was racing again. Placing a fake smile on my face, I resumed shopping for dinner. How was I going to do this with everyone keeping an eye on me? I looked around and saw no one. Grabbing one of the boxes in front of me, I quickly shoved it into my bag and quickly walked to the next isle.

"Emily, how are you doing?"

"As well as can be expected, Rick," I said, turning to give him a half smile.

"I heard. I am sorry for all the trouble you are going through."

"Thank you." What was he doing, this was not normal behavior for him. And he knows that I heard the conversation he had with Adam.

"It is good to see you out and about, they say the quickest way to get over loss is to get back to your regular routine."

"I know that was meant to be comforting, but it's not," I said, getting irritated. His eyes kept shifting. I had made him uncomfortable.

"I guess I should let you get back to—"

"Yes, please," I said, cutting him off. He quickly walked away from me. I calmed down again, taking deep breaths. My phone rang…Adam.

"Hello?"

"Hey, I, umm…"

"You were calling to check up on me?"

"N-no, well…maybe."

"I am mostly fine," I said, irritated again.

"Mostly? What's wrong?"

"What isn't wrong, Adam, I feel like an animal in a zoo, everyone is watching me. Are you checking up on me? Even Rick was oddly nice when he stopped me for a conversation. I am just trying to get the shopping done and this is just…" I couldn't stop myself from getting mad. If I thought people were staring at me before, I really had everyone staring at me now.

"Emily—"

"Don't, I'm fine," I said, cutting him off, and then hung up the phone. Grabbing my purse, I headed to the washroom, leaving the cart in the middle of the isle. I guess that it wasn't the worst thing that could have happened. So far so good, I guess. Not to mention a most believable mental breakdown in the middle of the store worked out well with giving me some time to figure out the rest of this. Taking a deep breath, I opened my purse and took out the pink box.

Chapter 12

As I waited, I stared at myself in the mirror, praying. I needed this to work out. I needed one thing to go right. Everything else in my life may be falling apart. Please, let this not be another thing to worry about.

"Is everything okay in there?" a voice asked on the other side of the door.

"It's fine, I just needed a minute." I hid the box in the garbage under a bunch of the paper towels and put the test in my purse. I splashed some more water on my face and opened the door. There were people hovering around the door and one stormed past me, basically shoving me out the door.

"Emily…" I heard Adam call from the front of the store.

"What?" I said, making sure to sound angry.

"I—"

"You got a call from all the nosy people that can't mind their own damn business," I said, raising my voice.

"It's not like that."

"Really, then what is it like? None of these people gave a damn when my mom died, or when my dad died."

"That is not true, and you know it. Your dad meant a lot to this town."

"And now that I am the only one left, and your chance is just narrowed down to one option, now is when everyone cares. But not about me. They only care what happens to YOU," I spewed out, not listening to him. I glared at him and then at all the other people that had stopped to stare.

"Emily, that is not—"

"Adam, it is, don't lie or try to cover it up. All of this, since I got back to town, has been all about you. I am leaving; I am done with all of this. I refuse to be a part of your sick twisted game that you insist on playing. I thought I was honoring my parents, and my grandparents, but the things you are doing to the children and what you make them go through with their siblings is cruel. At this point, why not just kill the second child at birth, make it so the kid doesn't even know they had a sibling. That way, you don't have to watch that child grow up, just to—" I couldn't continue. With all the rage inside and the hurt, I stormed past the crowd. Tears blurred my vision as I made my way to my car.

"Emily," Adam called, running up behind me and grabbing my arm.

"Let me go," I said, trying to pull myself free. "Adam, let's just go, right now. We can drive to the city now, not pack a thing."

"No," he said, angrier than I have ever seen him, "what the hell were you thinking? They are not supposed to know…" he said, ignoring the part about us leaving.

"Adam, save it. It's done, now the truth is out, this can stop."

"You have done nothing, they will tell them all an excuse of why you are acting this way, maybe overcome with grief for losing your sister, and things will continue as normal. But you've just—"

"I know what I have done, Adam. I know I have condemned myself to die. But it is better than this, my family will no longer be a part of this. It ends with me," I said, determined.

"So that means—"

"Yeah, Adam. I'm sorry. I know what this will mean for you, and I am sorrier than you will ever know. But I can't do this."

"Yeah, I was worried that it would turn out this way." He sighed and gave a nod. Before I could turn around, something hit the back of my head and I fell to the ground, a blurry image stepped over me and…I passed out.

When I regained consciousness, I was back in bed. I leapt up and winced at the pain from my head. I dressed quickly and opened the door, only to find Adam waiting on the other side of the door with a tray of food.

"What happened? Where is he?" I yelled.

"Who?"

"I saw—"

"Emily, you hit your head really hard. You should sit down and eat." There was something in his voice, the gentleness he spoke to me with before was gone. He was…angry? No…maybe…

"I did not hit my head, someone hit me, after you told him to."

"Emily, stop, YOU HIT YOUR HEAD. I can't make it any clearer, there was no one else there. You were rambling in the store, I helped you outside, you fell, hit your head."

"The store…my purse…" I started to panic; did he know?

"I dropped your purse off at the door. Why?"

"Oh, nothing, just worried if I lost it. With everything that happened last night, would hate to add missing ID to it too."

"So, are you good?" he asked suspiciously.

"I…Yeah…I'm sorry, Adam, I don't know—"

"It's okay, Emily, you're fine. It will be okay. I had a feeling that it would be too soon for you to go out last night."

"Yeah, I guess you were right. Thank you for looking out for me." I restrained myself from yelling at him, that I know what happened, that he was lying to me.

"So…Emily, to make sure it doesn't happen again, I am going to ask you for your car keys…just until we can make sure you are okay."

"Adam, I'm—"

"Emily, please don't make this harder than it has to be. Not to mention, I still have to go pick it up from the store 'cause I drove you home in my truck last night," Adam's voice was getting harder. More forceful.

"Fine, where is my purse?"

"I'll go get it." Within a couple minutes, he was back and handing me my purse. I opened the side pocket and handed him my keys. I placed the purse on the bed and grabbed the orange juice from the tray Adam brought into the room. My mind was scrambling for ideas to get him out of the room. I had to know.

"Adam…thank you," I said, looking him in the eyes. "I know I have been acting a bit crazy. I'm sorry." He looked at me as if contemplating if I was being sincere. "I thought I was over what happened to Ray, and all this weird stuff happening. You were right to try and stop me from going to the store yesterday, and for checking up on me. It was all too much, and I should have known better than that to act like it was all just normal. I didn't allow myself to freak out, and I didn't realize how much it was all affecting me." I saw his eyes soften a bit, but he still didn't speak. "If it is all right with you, could I rest a bit longer?" He nodded and left the room. I ate slowly, waiting to see if he would return. After a little while, I finally heard his footsteps leading away from the door. I slowly opened my purse and felt around, keeping an eye on the door. As I grabbed hold of the pregnancy test, I allowed myself to close my eyes and quickly prayed. When I opened my eyes, my heart dropped, looking at the test that read positive. I was pregnant. My hand went to my stomach and I started crying.

"I'm sorry," I whispered. Wait…it might be okay; I gave myself a little hope. It is just one, the curse won't take into effect if I don't have a second child. But to find out more, Adam and the doctor would know. What would happen if they knew? But Adam should know, he's the father. My head was spinning, and I barely made it to the washroom, before I threw up all the food I had just eaten. Sure enough, Adam was right behind me. It was inevitable that he would find out. And it probably should be sooner than later.

"Are you all right?" he said, still sounding distant.

"Yeah, I'll be fine." I ran a glass of water from the tap and drank it. Should I tell him? Yes, he should know. "Come with me, I want to show you something." He looked at me hesitantly.

"I promise you'll like it," I said, smiling. I reached out my hand to him. He followed me, but did not take my hand. I walked slowly, trying to muster up the strength to appear happier. When we finally reached my bedroom, he suspiciously looked around and then saw the test lying on the bed. His eyes widened as he saw the results.

"Emily…I…oh my god…This is great. No wonder you've been all over the place." All suspicion had left and was replaced by pure joy. He grabbed me into his arms and lifted me off the floor. Okay, one problem down. Adam was back to normal. Now just had to figure out how to deal with the rest of it. "Was this why you wanted to cook me a special dinner, did you know?"

"I…hoped I was," I said, trying to sound like I was happy about it.

That night, Adam cooked me a special dinner. The food was amazing, at least there was one thing I didn't have to fake that night. My head was spinning, how was I going to leave? That had to be my number-one priority. The baby would wait, it is not like I was giving birth in the next few days. I have time to think about that later. Maybe I could talk to Adam and we could both leave together. Maybe I could get him to listen.

"Emily?"

"Hmm?" I said, realizing he was trying to get my attention.

"Hey, what are you thinking about?" he said, grabbing my hand, running his thumb over the top.

"The future, the baby, you? Honestly, my head is kind of overwhelmed right now." Being honest with him felt like the best thing right now. Can't have him getting suspicious again. I would have to feel out when was the right time to ask him, but it wasn't right now.

"I'll be here, you don't have to worry. I will get you through this." I smiled slightly.

"Thank you, Adam."

"Come on, let's get you back to bed. You need to rest." I didn't argue; I let him lead me back upstairs. He didn't look like he was going to leave.

"Adam, you realize, if you stay, resting is going to be the farthest thing from my mind, right?" I said, seductively stepping closer to him smiling. He smirked and kissed me before leaving the room.

A couple days later, Adam's mom died in an accidental death at home. Between funeral arrangements and work, I barely got to see Adam. He suggested that I don't go with all the stress I have been under. I couldn't disagree. I haven't been sleeping well, have been having morning sickness,

119

and my head wouldn't stop trying to figure out how to get myself out of this situation. After the funeral, Adam came over to check up on me. We talked for a while until he said he was tired and needed to lay down. I made myself a cup of tea and sat on the porch.

Okay. Let's start figuring this out. I could pretend to go for a walk, but if anyone saw me, they would bring me back, and there was no way I could outrun a town of people conspiring to keep this ritual going. I couldn't drive, Adam took my keys. Although, if I managed to get him to let me know where they were, that would be a lot easier, though I'm not sure I would be able to get him to trust me enough for that. My mind wandered from thoughts of trying to get away to thoughts of Adam. We have known each other for a long time, and he has always been the helpful friendly type. Since James and Ben, I have seen...sides of him that I didn't like. The manipulative, the competitive. Just...but could I really blame him? He just wanted to survive. Wait a minute? How did he know...? His mom...? But that would mean, that it wasn't me...maybe...the rest weren't either. I know I heard Adam say it was, but what if he didn't know either? Maybe he just thought it was because he didn't do it. Or maybe he did, and just wanted Rick to think it was me? After all, he did say it was him that did it when I talked to him. Or was he lying then just so that I wouldn't think it was me?

I went to go lay down, but the thoughts weren't stopping, who was I kidding? I would never get to sleep thinking about all of this. I got back up and went to look for Adam. I found him on the couch, asleep in front of the dimming fire. I watched as he slept. He looked happy, peaceful. I couldn't help but think how handsome he was. If not for any of this with my sister, I might have actually fallen in lo—

"Emily, is everything okay...?" Adam said, waking up, watching me looking at him.

"Oh yeah, I couldn't sleep."

"Come here," he said, reaching for my hand.

"Actually, I was wondering if maybe we could go for a walk. I'm kind of restless, but I didn't want you to worry if I went on my own. But if you're tired—"

"No, it's fine, we can do that," he said, pushing himself off the couch. I grabbed my shoes and a sweater. Adam was ready a little while later. We started down the path beside the lake.

"Adam..." I started hesitantly.

"What is it?" he said, talking my hand as we kept walking.

"Would you actually go through with the ritual if we had two kids?"

"You mean, would I pick one over the other and sentence one to die?"

"Yeah, I guess that is what I am asking."

"Well, look at it this way. Do you want both kids to die at 30 by not telling them? This way, at least one would have a way to live. Also, who's to say we couldn't make an arrangement with one of the other families and have both of them survive?"

"You mean like your brother and uncle? Or what your mom did for you?"

"That, or like almost all the families have tried to do. Most haven't worked, of course. They were way too subtle."

"Subtle, meaning?"

"Like what our parents did with us, introducing us so young, hoping something might happen. They, of course, didn't know that after your mom's death, you wouldn't want to stay in town when they did it, but—"

"After she died, Ray and Dad started pulling away, and it just got hard…"

"I am not blaming you, just when you kept coming back for the summer, Mom realized that it would take more than subtle to keep me alive."

"Adam…did…"

"Emily, you can ask me anything. If I don't want to tell you the answer, I will tell you that." I took a deep breath.

"Did you ever actually want to be with me, or was it just first 'cause that was what your parents wanted and then to live? How many before me and Ray did you try with?"

"Three before you, but I didn't want to, it was also before I knew about any of this. It was more my mom trying to set me up and was hoping it would work without telling me."

"And the first question?" He stopped walking and turned away from me, but didn't let go of my hand.

"When you came back, even before all this, I have wanted you. I've tried not to 'cause I knew you were with James, so I avoided you as much as I could. I was jealous as hell that you would be with someone like him. I really have wanted you for a long time, not so much when we were kids, it was after. You came out for the summers and would leave, your dad would be upset, and I would come out to talk to him. I guess that I started wanting you to stay longer at first for his benefit. I didn't understand then why you would leave him alone all the time, even as a teenager, I couldn't understand why you and your sister would put him in so much pain. As I grew up, it was easier, but I noticed myself getting angrier each time you would leave him all by himself. This was before I knew about any of this of course. I found myself wondering why I was getting so mad about it. At first, I thought that it was because I thought of your father like family, checking up on him, making sure he was okay. Then I realized it was more. I saw something different in you. You were never the flashy girl who needed attention, like Raylene, or half the other girls in this town that threw themselves at every available guy. You honestly didn't seem like you needed anyone. Maybe that was what started drawing me to you. I started talking to your dad about you more and more. At first, it was just asking about you, what you were up to when you were not here. As he told me more, I found myself wanting to talk to you to find out about you from you, not just from your dad. After your dad died, even knowing you were with James, I came out here to check up on the place and was wishing you would see me. After your dad died, and it might sound creepy, but I came out here at times when I was upset and pretend…we were together…and you would be here trying to cheer me up. As time went by, you distanced yourself when you came here, started staying at the cabin more instead of heading to town. It was harder to talk to you. You weren't staying as long either. Anyway, once the three didn't work out and since my 30th birthday is getting close, Mom decided to tell me everything she knew, which still isn't a whole lot 'cause no one really talks about it, I have only known about this for the last few months. Emily, I can't say that I am sorry for how things have turned out for you 'cause that would have meant that we would not have had a chance together. And any time with you was worth it for me." He turned back to me and looked at me hopefully.

"Can we keep walking?" I asked. He looked at me expectantly, wanting me to say more, but I couldn't. So, after searching my face for a minute, he simply nodded. We continued to walk. We were almost all the way around the lake.

"Okay," I said softly, finally breaking the silence.

"Okay???" he asked.

"You're right, your mom has helped us out with this and there should be no reason for you to die as well, so, okay, I will marry you. With the condition that we only have one child. This child," I said, pulling his hand to my stomach. "If we only have one, then this circle won't have to keep going. With only one child, we don't have to sacrifice one. The one child can grow up normal, never even having to know of the ritual." He stopped walking again, this time turning to me.

"Emily…I am not sure it will work…but I am willing to try."

"So, when do you turn 30?"

"In a couple of weeks."

"Wow, that is really close. No wonder you were getting desperate."

"Yeah, is that okay?"

"Sure…Let's get married tomorrow, small and simple." Adam's eyes lit up.

"Really?"

"Really. Why wait, 1 day or 14, the few days won't make a big difference. I don't have any family left; it won't be hard to get your family to agree. We do this tomorrow and then we can start working on the rest."

"The rest?"

"Carrying on where your mom left off. And before you say anything, no, I will follow the rules. I won't put the baby in danger. But I don't want this to continue for our child. I don't want one of the other families thinking they can keep doing things the same and get our child involved again. There has to be a way to stop this."

"Emily, please, what if you looking for a way out—"

"Adam, I know what you are going to say, and I am sorry, but I have to. Too many people are dying. And we will continue to die because of this. But let's start with you. You are one life we know we can save, so we will start with you." Adam gave me a hesitant smile, and slowly nodded.

"Okay, so I guess I won't be able to stop you, but as long as you promise the baby will be safe."

"I promise. I'll be careful. But, Adam, I need you to know. Things might not go back to how they were before."

"You mean with us?" he asked, looking disappointed.

"Yeah, it's just, so much has happened and then everything with Ray...even after you knew what happened with James, I—"

"Yeah, Emily, I am really sorry about all that. I shouldn't have."

"You were trying to make your mom's death mean something..."

"I know, and I understand why you are feeling the way you are about me. So, I guess, thank you. You could easily just let the two weeks pass and I could be—"

"Adam, don't. I might not feel the way I did toward you that I did before, but I can't have another person that I care about, die. Actually, now that I think about it, you are the last person that I care about left alive." Adam stared at me. I think he finally understood why I wanted to stop the ritual. To have it end with me. Adam would still have his dad, his uncle, his sister from his family still left alive, even if his mom did sacrifice herself. I have lost everyone; even in the city, there was no one that I was particularly close to. The closest ones would be James's parents, but that was kind of in the past. There is no way they would ever want to speak to me again. Adam reached his hand out and wiped a tear from my cheek. I didn't even notice that I started crying.

"Do you think you are ready to sleep?" I took a deep breath and shook my head.

"No, but if you need to sleep, I am all right with heading home."

"Well, how 'bout we head back, and I make you some hot chocolate?" I nodded.

"Hey, Adam, if I were to ask you to move back to the city with me, would you? Never tell our child of this place."

"But at 30, the journal said no deviations?"

"Well, that is just a thought. The ritual doesn't start until a piece of wooden item created by both people is added to the cabin. When I had that dream vision thing of my dad, he said it was already too late for Ray and I, but what if it is as simple as never telling our child about the ritual, we could move—"

"Emily, I…" he looked scared.

"Look, you don't need to decide now, just…just could you think about it?" He stayed silent, but nodded.

A short time later, we were seated in the cabin in front of the fireplace, with hot chocolate in hand.

"Emily…" Adam said, breaking the silence.

"Yeah."

"Thank you."

"For what?"

"For going through with this, for literally saving my life. I know I messed up with…with Raylene, but I am still very grateful that you would do something like this." I gave him a half smile. I didn't know how to reply. I finished my hot chocolate, said goodnight, and headed for bed. I tossed and turned for a bit, but finally managed to get some sleep. By the time I woke up the next day, Adam had already dressed up in a suit and had gone to town and bought me a dress. He was just finishing making breakfast. I managed to eat a piece of toast and drink a quarter cup of orange juice before there was a knock on the door.

On the other side was Adam's dad, and uncle as well, as the preacher following behind them. There were a couple of others that Adam was close to, that Adam also invited. Adam thought bringing everyone here would be easier on me than taking me into town. I got dressed in the dress Adam bought for me. As I was leaving the bathroom, a wave of nausea hit and I rushed back in, closing the door behind me, but not soon enough, Adam's uncle saw me. When I emerged from the bathroom, Rick was scrutinizing me closely.

"There she is, I was beginning to think you were getting cold feet," Adam's dad said warmly.

"No, sir, no cold feet," I said, plastering a big smile on my face. "I'm just going to grab some water." Adam followed close behind.

"Everything okay?"

"Yeah, just a little nauseous," I said with a weak smile.

"Well, as much as I don't like that you are not feeling well...I can't say that I mind too much in this particular case," he said, coming up behind me and wrapping his arms around my waist, slowly running his hands along my stomach. I smiled.

"Yeah, I can't say I mind either." Suddenly, aware of how close Adam was, I took his hands off my stomach. "Umm, we should—"

"Yeah, sorry," he said, looking at me apologetically.

"It's fine, this child is yours too, it just...Too soon." Adam nodded.

"It's okay, Emily, you don't have to explain, but I do–"

"Hey, you two ready to get this started?" Adam and I turned to look at Rick standing in the doorway. Adam grabbed my hand.

"We just need one more moment," Adam said quickly. Rick eyed us but nodded and left. "So, for appearances' sake...umm...the kiss."

"Adam, it's fine. I was aware that it is part of getting married," I said, smiling. He nodded, and as we headed out, I could see him smiling.

It was a sweet, simple ceremony. Adam's family looked really happy. With tears streaming down his father's face, he grabbed me for a hug.

"Thank you for doing this for him," he said, whispering in my ear.

"All right, let's toast to the happy couple," Rick said, handing everyone a glass of champagne. I took the glass he handed me and set it down on the mantle of the fireplace.

"Before we do that," Adam said, "There is something we would like to tell you." Adam looked at me, grinning for ear to ear. "Emily is pregnant." A chorus of cheers erupted, followed by lots of congratulations and hand shaking.

After we all ate dinner and spent a couple more hours socializing, Adam found me outside.

"There you are."

"Yeah, sorry, just getting a bit tired, needed some fresh air."

"I understand, my family can be a bit much, loving to the point of suffocation." We chuckled. "Want me to kick them out?" I looked at him wide-eyed.

"I appreciate the thought but I can't ask you to do that. They are your family and are happy for you."

"Look, Emily, you are my wife, pregnant with my child, and from now on, you are the person that I want to make happy. I may have screwed up a lot on the way but I can't change that now. The only think I can do is try to make it up to you, maybe hope that one day you can forgive me and if that means kicking everyone out, just say the word." I couldn't help but smile at how sweet his speech was.

"What?" he asked, noting the smile on my face.

"You are very sweet, Adam. I mean, I already knew that but it is still sweet."

"Sooo…"

"So, I guess that people generally don't have receptions at their house, so they don't have to make things awkward."

"True, so if you don't want me to kick them out, what would you like to do?"

"Can we—"

"Let me guess, you want to get out of here?" I nodded. "And since you are tired, you want to go for a drive?" I nodded again. "But you are worried that suggesting going somewhere with me, that I might take it the wrong way?" I nodded again. "Let's go." I followed him.

"Thank you," I said, when we were driving down a dirt road.

"Emily, I told you. I will do anything to make you happy. Are you feeling better?"

"Well, I am still tired but better. Hey, Adam…without taking it the wrong way, could you drive to that spot you took me to the last day we hung out together?" He looked at me questioningly but did a U-turn. We didn't speak for the drive up the hill or the short hike.

"You know, for being tired, you're making me look bad," he said, slightly out of breath.

"Sorry," I said with a half-smile, looking back at him, as he was trying to keep up.

"Yeah, sure you are," he said, smirking back. "Should I be worried that you wanted to come here?"

"No, I'm okay. I am not going to do anything stupid. I promised, remember?" I said, taking his hand and placing it on my stomach.

"I understand, sorry. Just—"

"I know." At the end of the dirt trail, Adam stopped. I gave his hand a squeeze and continued up the path that had now turned rocky. Carefully climbing the rocks as I had done so many times before, I understood why Adam was worried about me wanting to come out here. The last day we were out here together, I had told him how bad things were with my dad, my mom was dead, and Raylene had left. I had looked over the edge of the cliff and remembered asking him if he ever thought of jumping. I remember him having to practically drag me down the hill, and on the drive home, he asked if there was another way I thought I could get what I wanted without actually jumping. The very next day, I left. At the time, I didn't care where I was going and when I settled in the city, I did let my dad know where I was. I learned about this place years before my mother died. She would bring me up here to tell me of the story of the day she brought Dad up here for a picnic and told him she was pregnant. She remembered how happy she was and then, told me so many stories as we sat on the rocks up there. Sitting on the top after she died, it was the only place I felt close to her. The only times I remember her truly happy was when she brought me here. She seemed sad a lot of the time. I knew she was trying to hide it even then, but as I got older, I noticed it more and more. Knowing what I know now, I finally understood.

I don't know how long I stayed up there, but with tears streaming down my face, I made my way back down to where Adam waited. I ran up to him and buried my face in his shoulder and cried. He stayed with his arms wrapped around me until I was able to regain my composure. He helped me slowly back to the car and drove home.

Rick's vehicle was still in the driveway at the cabin.

"Stay here, I'll tell him to go home." I nodded, and Adam left. It was a while before he came out. Glaring at me, he got in his vehicle and took off. I got out and headed into the cabin.

"Emily, I am sorry," Adam said, trying to tidy up some of the mess.

"Adam, don't worry about it, it was a celebration. It was bound to get a little messy. I'm going to shower." He nodded and continued cleaning. After getting out, I helped Adam clean for a bit.

"You should get some rest; you were tired hours ago."

"Adam." I finally stopped cleaning and looked at him. He looked at me, concerned.

"What is it? I had a feeling something was wrong when you were up there, but I didn't want to push you."

"I know, and believe me, I appreciate that you know me well enough to know that I needed time to process things before I can talk about it." I paused and took a deep breath. "Adam, I think my mom did what yours did for you." His eyes grew wide.

"Are you sure?"

"I'm not 100% sure yet. When I went up there, I started remembering some of the stories she told me on those picnics. I remembered thinking she should write books 'cause they were so entertaining. I remembered trying to get Mom to tell them to Ray, but she said they were just for me." I started to cry again. Adam took my hand and led me to the couch and held me.

"I don't remember all the stories, but I remembered pieces of each story and if I put them together, they actually start sounding like she was trying to warn me. Adam, I killed my mom."

"No, it was her choice. You didn't know."

"Adam, your mom did the same for you. Are you saying you don't feel the least bit guilty?" He thought for a while.

"Okay, so I see your point. I guess I do feel sort of responsible."

"Is this what is going to happen with us too?"

"What do you mean?"

"Say we have two kids. You said you would go through with it. How would you decide which one gets to live? And then, if we couldn't live with letting either of them die, one of us would sacrifice our lives to save the child. Giving them a fair shot to live. So, in the end, one parent always dies 'cause no parent would be able to go through with it. And let's put the odds at 50 percent, that even if told, they might find another of the 11 families to marry. So only one child would marry who they want, the other would marry out of necessity, or they won't marry and die. Adam, none of this seems fair. And for what? Just so the families never have to worry about money or health issues or any of the other stuff, but is it worth it, if literally half the family dies each generation?"

"Emily, what other choice is there?"

"Well, I know it is too late for us. But we could leave." I looked at him pleadingly.

"Emily, it's late, let's save this conversation for another day. It is our wedding; we are both going to live. So, for now, we are doing okay. Right?" I nodded. A little discouraged, he was trying to avoid talking about us leaving again. I decided to leave it for a while; maybe I'll try talking about it in a few weeks.

Chapter 13

The next few days were organizing and sorting for me while Adam was moving his stuff into the cabin. Once he unloaded the truck of the last of his stuff, he went back to work. A few days later, Adam brought me to the doctor to get me checked out and make sure things were going okay with the baby.

I was starting to feel better about the whole situation, getting into the new routine with Adam. Unfortunately, the doctor's visit turned all that upside down again.

"You haven't said anything the whole way home, is everything okay with the baby?" Adam asked, concerned.

"Adam, I thought I could do this. I am not sure I can anymore."

"What do you mean?"

"I was fine when we were only having one child. I would be able to stop getting pregnant a second time, but now—"

"Wait, are you telling me—"

"Twins," I said, tearing up. "Adam, kids are supposed to be happy news and I really want to be, but I can't help but think about their future and the pain they will go through."

"Emily, there is still a lot of time between now and then, they are not even born yet and until they are at least starting to get involved with people, we don't need to worry. We will figure something out."

"Okay." I tried to appear happier, but couldn't manage a whole lot. I could tell Adam was really happy. He would have to be happy for the both of us.

"Come on, let me take you out for dinner and cheer you up." I smiled and nodded.

A while later, in the middle of dinner, I noticed someone in the back of the restaurant.

"Adam?"

"Yeah?"

"What is with your uncle? I don't think he approves of your choice of wife?" After a period of silence, he finally spoke.

"He doesn't." His truthfulness shocked me at first. "He says you are too much like your mother and he is concerned."

"About?"

"About your outburst in the supermarket, about the fact that you are trying to leave. The fact that our marriage is not—"

"Wait, have you been talking to him about us?"

"Emily, I don't have to talk to anyone. This is a small town, and everyone knows everyone's business. What brought this on?"

"Because he is staring me down from across the room and I don't know why. Since the wedding, I have seen him a few times, and each time, it is the same." Adam followed my gaze to the table Rick was sitting at. After Rick saw that Adam noticed him, he got up and left.

"I'll have a talk with him, you don't have to worry about him."

"Adam, I think there are things you are not telling me. I haven't figured out why, if it is that you are trying to protect me or you think I can't handle the truth, I don't know…But if it affects me or the babies, will you tell me?" He looked shocked, but slowly nodded.

"As I said, you have nothing to worry about. My priority is you. If anything is threatening your safety, I will deal with it. I won't let anything happen to you."

"Adam, can we go?" I said after a moment of silence.

"Yeah, that probably is a good idea."

I headed to bed shortly after getting home. I woke up a little while later to Adam arguing with someone. I carefully made my way to the window. Rick's truck. I opened the door and stood at the top of the stairs.

"You need to watch your back, Adam, this one is unpredictable like her mother. The last thing you want is for this to go sideways."

"It already is sideways. The bodies are piling up and now, you are freaking Emily out more."

"Well, someone has to keep an eye on her."

"I am," Adam yelled.

"No, you aren't. You have been blind when it comes to her. She is dangerous and if you want my advice, get rid of her as soon as those babies are born."

"Rick, you need to leave. That is my wife you are threatening."

"Man, she has you wrapped around her little finger. For not getting anything out of this marriage, you are head over heels for her. That makes you one of the stupid ones. I thought your dad and I taught you better."

"Rick, just go, what happens now is no longer your concern, everyone got what they wanted."

"You are foolish if you think you can control her," Rick said, getting angrier.

"Keep your voice down, do you want her to hear you?"

"Adam, you don't have to decide today. It is not like I am telling you to harm your children, but your wife will be a problem, even if not today, she will be."

"Rick, go, and don't come anywhere near my wife again." I hurried quietly back to my room and watched out the window, waiting for Rick to leave. Would Adam listen to him? Or would Rick come after me himself? I tried to get back to sleep that night. I couldn't. I found Adam asleep on the couch in front of the fireplace.

"Sorry, I didn't mean to wake you," I said, when I noticed his eyes open.

"Can't sleep?"

"No…Adam, I heard you and Rick talking."

"Emily, you have to know I wouldn't do it," he said, looking panicked. "I kicked him out; I told him not to come near you again."

"I know. I heard. But would he do it himself?"

"I don't know," he said, not meeting my eyes, "But I won't let him hurt you, you have to know that." He stood up and grabbed my shoulders, looking me directly in my eyes. "I promise, even after our babies are born, I will protect you if he tries anything." I didn't know what to say, not sure how I should react. So, I did the only thing I could. I buried my head into his shoulder and my arms around his waist. Adam hugged me back tightly.

"Adam, why are you always sleeping on the couch?"

"Well, James went nuts in one of the rooms, and Ben in the other, so I would rather not stay in them. Just in case. Also, if anyone were to come into the cabin, those rooms are farther down the hall from yours, which means yours would be the first one someone would enter, so I would rather put myself in front of your room than farther back." I couldn't stop myself from smiling.

"Come on," I said, leading him to the bedroom.

"Are you sure?"

"You are my husband and have been sleeping on the couch for weeks. The least I can do is let you sleep in a bed. Besides, I think, knowing Rick wants me…out of the way, I would prefer you closer. That is if you want to."

"Are you kidding, a bed sounds great. And sleeping next to you sounds even better." Having Adam next to me made me feel safer. I don't know why, but I believed him. I knew he would never hurt me. He would keep us all safe.

After three weeks of routine, I decided to ask Adam again if we could leave.

"Emily, you already said it is too late for us," he said, not meeting my eyes.

"Yes, but it doesn't have to be for them."

"I told you I would help you find a loophole, Emily, but we can't just take off. You said before, the house wouldn't let you when you tried before." As much as I didn't want to admit it, he was probably right. I guess the only reason nothing has happened is because Adam hadn't been convinced to leave.

"Okay, so what are your thoughts?"

"I don't have any yet. Maybe we could go through the journals again."

"Sure, where are they?"

"I thought you were the last one to go through them?"

"The last time I saw them was before Ray was…" I couldn't finish the sentence.

"Actually, come to think of it, I haven't seen them since then either." We spent most of the day looking everywhere we could think of for them. I made Adam check the room under the floor; I couldn't go back down there. I couldn't help but wonder if Adam was actually trying to help me or if he was asking about the journals to get rid of them, like Rick wanted him to. Even though I knew Adam would not hurt me, he already admitted that he would continue the ritual.

When Adam left for work the next day, I sat down at the kitchen table and started writing out all the things I could think of to help figure out how to break the ritual. The first one would be to not start it. Don't get pregnant. But since that was already off the table, what else could I do? The music box linked to the ritual; I wonder? I walked to the fireplace and grabbed the music box off the mantle. I opened it. The melody disrupted the quiet morning, and usually I would think it was soothing, but not today. I closed the lid and taking a deep breath, while hoping it would work, I threw it into the dying fire. I stoked the fire to get it going a bit. The outside started to turn black, but would not catch fire. I threw another piece of wood on the fire and it caught fire almost immediately. The music box didn't. I maneuvered the burning wood on top of the music box. My heart sank as I watched the log burn, but not the box. I put a few more logs on the fire, surrounding the box.

I went back to the table and started writing down all the other ways I might be able to destroy the box. Though, if trying to burn wood didn't work, I wasn't holding much hope that any of the others would either. But I had to try. My other option was trying to find my car keys and leaving town without Adam, I could do it while he was at work. Okay. So, continue trying to destroy the music box or leave without Adam. I couldn't risk making him suspicious again by talking about any of this, and he made it clear he wouldn't leave with me. I looked at the time and realized Adam would be home soon. I had spent all day doing this and made no progress. I gathered up my papers and hid them in the guest bedroom under the mattress. I checked the fireplace and found what I already knew I would find, the wood all burned to ash, and the blackened but not burned music box. I fished it out. It fell off the shovel, instinctively I reached out for it.

I was expecting to be burned, but it was barely warm. Adam walked in while I was cleaning up the ashes that had spilled.

"Hey, is there anything you want to tell me?" Adam asked, seeing the blackened music box on the coffee table behind me.

"Oh, that. I was trying to see if I could nullify the contract, so to speak. You can see how well that turned out." Adam smiled at me. "What's that look for, it isn't funny."

"All right, I'll bite. Let's try to destroy a music box." I looked at him, shocked that he would agree so quickly. We took the box outside; he tried a sledgehammer…and smashed it.

"Really. It wouldn't burn, but it broke with one swing?" Adam laughed as he flexed. I gave him a playful shove when something caught my eye. Adam's gaze followed mine. The music box was repairing itself. And, in less than a minute, it was back to how it was before I burned it.

"Well, that is something you don't see every day." Not knowing what else to do, we took the box in the house and set it back on the mantle. A while later, we were sitting, eating dinner.

"What if we didn't let it repair. Split up the pieces?" I asked. Without saying anything, Adam left the room, I followed. He picked up the music box and took it back outside. Raising the sledgehammer above his head, he sent it crashing down on the box. It didn't break. Not even a dent was made in the box this time. I watched as Adam tried a couple more times, without success.

"Adam, it's okay," I said, grabbing his arm before he could swing again.

"I'm sorry," he said, sounding sincere. I grabbed him around the waist and kissed him. He released his grip on the sledgehammer and pulled me closer.

"I want you to know how much it means to me that you would try," I said, pulling back a bit.

"Emily, I told you I would." I nodded, picking up the music box.

"I told you she would do this," Rick said, coming out of the bushes. Adam changed his position to place himself between me and Rick.

"Adam, I won't harm your wife," Rick said, glaring at me. "She is still pregnant after all. I just want to talk." Adam looked at me; I gave him a slight nod. He and Rick headed to the kitchen and I put the music box on the mantle. The discussion got loud very quickly, but through the door, I couldn't make out any of the words. When I opened the door, Rick turned to stare at me.

"You have no idea what you are doing, don't think that just 'cause you are married this makes everything fine. You are putting Adam in danger, every time you pull him into trying something like this." I looked at him, puzzled, but said nothing. He stormed past me, shoving me into the wall.

"Rick, that is enough," Adam yelled. With one last look toward Adam and then to me, Rick stormed out of the cabin.

"You okay?" Adam asked. I nodded. "We should get some sleep; it's been a long day." As we lay in bed, I could hear Adam breathing behind me. I rolled over to face him to find him staring at me.

"Adam, what's wrong?"

"Nothing," he said, turning to lay on his back. The moonlight from the window let me see his face enough to let me know he was lying. I sat up and took his hand.

"Adam, please, tell me what's wrong." He looked at me with a pained expression in his eyes.

"I...I think...maybe Rick might be right?" I couldn't help but look shocked. "No, Emily, not all of it," he said, quickly sitting up. "Just the part about me..." He took a deep breath before continuing. "Being so completely in love with you that I am risking everything to try and help you without thinking about the consequences for my safety."

"I understand. It's okay, we don't have to continue." It was his turn to be shocked. "Like you said, we have 30 years before this will affect our kids. We have a lot of time to make some wonderful memories."

"Emily, you don't know how happy you have just made me—" He stopped. "What is it?" He leaned in and kissed me softly.

"You have no idea how much I want you right now," he said, whispering.

"Then maybe you should show me," I said, smiling at him.

"Are you sure?"

"Adam," I said, looking him in the eyes. "I am human, you are my husband. Not to mention, you are an incredibly handsome man half naked in my bed." With a smile on his face, he leaned in for another kiss.

A while later, I looked over at Adam sleeping peacefully, a few rays of light streamed in through the window. I carefully got out of bed so I wouldn't wake him up. When I got downstairs, I started by checking Adam's coat, no car keys, his truck keys lay on the stand next to the grandfather clock. I grabbed them and went outside. As quickly as I could, I searched the cab of the truck everywhere I could think of. Of course, I found them in the last spot I could think of, the ashtray. I grabbed the keys and tried to put everything back as I found it. I hurried back into the house, placing his truck keys where I found them. I heard Adam moving around upstairs and quickly went to the kitchen. I started a pot of coffee and hid the car keys under one of the coffee mugs in the back of the cupboard, then started making breakfast. As I was plating, Adam walked in, grinning at me. I set the plates down and poured him a cup of coffee. As I was about to walk away, he pulled me onto his lap and kissed me.

"I love you so much, Emily," he said, when he pulled away.

"I...I need time, Adam. With everything with Ray, I...can't say it yet," I said, getting off his lap and getting me a glass of orange juice, then sat beside him at the table.

"Hey, it's okay. I know I hurt you and it is okay if you need time to trust me again. I just...I needed you to know. And I don't know if last night was a one-time thing, but I...Thank you." I smiled and kissed him again.

"I can't answer that yet either, but you should eat your breakfast, it is getting cold." He turned to his plate and started eating. After he left for work, I looked around the cabin and putting my hand on my stomach, I realized it was now or never. No stopping like last time, just had to drive. I grabbed the keys from where I hid them earlier and without packing anything, I grabbed my purse and left. I hoped Adam would forgive me, I thought as I sat in my car. I did care for him a lot, and he was right, I was being selfish to ask him to risk his life with mine. I started driving. I took one last look in the rearview mirror as the cabin disappeared out of view.

I breathed a sigh of relief as I picked up speed. Unfortunately, there was only one road out of town, and it went straight through the town. I knew I wasn't safe yet. As I drove by Adam's work, I saw him getting out of his truck and notice my car. I didn't stop. I saw him shaking his head as I drove by and climb back into his truck to follow me. He wasn't trying to catch me, he just followed. I was starting to get a bad feeling and then I saw it, there was a barricade across the road. I punched the steering wheel and winced at the pain that followed. Realizing that he knew all along what I was trying to do, I stopped the car, did a U-turn, and drove back home. I hid the keys in the music box hoping Adam wouldn't look in there, maybe I will find another chance to try again. I didn't have a lot of time. He pulled into the driveway shortly after I did.

"Why, Emily?" he asked, as soon as he walked in the door.

"Because you were right, I was putting you in danger and I wouldn't be able to live with myself if something happened to you. But I couldn't live with myself knowing I am sentencing one of our babies to die by staying. I thought that it would solve all the problems."

"Would you have told me where you were?" I couldn't meet his eyes.

"No, you would have brought me right back here."

"You're probably right." Adam looked hurt. "Emily…Are we ever going to be able to trust each other?"

"I don't know."

"I did mean what I said this morning, Emily, I do love you, but you need to stop. I don't want to lose you." He hesitated, but lifted my chin to look into his eyes. "Because I don't think I could live without you. So, please, no more trying to leave." I nodded. He kissed me and wrapped his arms around me.

Chapter 14

Later that night, I woke up and went to get some fresh air. I heard voices at the side of the house, and quietly walked over.

"Is it over?" Rick asked.

"For now, she said she wouldn't try to leave anymore."

"Do you believe her?"

"Not sure yet. It's not like she handed me the keys to prove to me she wouldn't."

"Well, I gotta hand it to you, Adam, you were right about all of it. I'm kind of impressed. From sleeping on the couch so she would ask you back into her bed, to telling her you couldn't live without her. I never thought that your way would work."

"Yeah, well, women are all the same, they like the feelings, and vulnerability in men. I will never understand why, but whatever works, right?"

"Yeah, but how do you do it?"

"What?"

"Make her believe you actually love her?"

"Women hear what they want to hear. Right now, Emily needed to believe that someone cared about her, so she was willing to accept that I did. Besides she is hot, it is very easy to pretend I love her, if I get sex out of it." Rick laughed.

"So, you going to finish it when your kids are born?"

"I don't have much of a choice, do I?"

"Not really, unless you get someone to do it for you."

"No, it should be me. After all, she did this to herself. If she wouldn't have gone digging, maybe we could have spared her for a bit."

"It is weird though, she found so much stuff out and yet, she still hasn't figured out this ritual is never about them, the women always cave," Rick said, Adam chuckled.

"Yeah they do. But at least in a few months, my part will be done when she is out of the way. Let's just hope she has two boys instead of girls, since the girls never survive." I couldn't listen anymore. I carefully made my way back inside and sat on the edge of my bed.

So this ritual was never meant for the women, the women usually cave first. So the mothers were meant to sacrifice each time, the ritual was for blood, just like Adam said a while ago. The more the better. But if the men were to live, how was it that Adam's sister was told about the ritual. Unless his mom did it to save them both, hoping. Maybe she didn't know the end game that her daughter would die anyway. So, siblings sacrificing each other, husbands sacrificing their wives. Parents sacrificing their children. All for a house that craved blood, just to enjoy a few perks while they are still alive. Who the hell was this damn ritual for? I heard the door open downstairs; I laid down and pretended to be asleep. A few minutes later, I heard Adam come into the room and felt him lay down next to me. He draped an arm across my body as he curled up beside me. I wanted to scream at him. I wanted to push him away, but I didn't. I pretended to sleep. He played me this whole time, everything he said, everything he did, it was to get me to do exactly what he wanted me to do. Blaming me for killing Raylene, all those conversations I overheard with Rick, he probably knew I was listening. How though? Come on, Emily, think. How would he know about all of it before I even knew what I was going to do? Rick, maybe he was spying on me? The house? If it was the house, how did the house know? The house can't read minds. Could it hear? See? Read body language?

Emily, calm down, he will notice you are awake. The spirits? No, the two that were here were trying to help me, they led me to the other journal. My mother's grave, they were trying to tell me…Actually, thinking about it, I haven't seen them lately. Not since Raylene was killed. Do they need two to show up, siblings who both know? I don't know who the angry man was, but the woman who wrote the journal, her name. What was her name? Maggie. Maybe the man was killed by his sibling and was stuck here too. Does that mean Raylene? Would she be stuck here now too? I didn't kill her, but if Adam did, I had to find out. I started to sniff quietly. I felt Adam's arm tighten around me. Bringing my hand up to my eyes, I pretended to wipe tears away, but instead, poked myself in the eye. Might as well make the tears real.

"Emily?" he whispered, concerned.

"Yeah," I said softly.

"Are you?"

"Oh, sorry," I said, turning to him now that the tears were flowing, "I didn't mean to wake you. I just had a dream about Ray." He wiped the tears from my eyes. "Adam, I heard you telling Rick a while ago that I killed her, but I know it wasn't me."

"You heard?" I nodded.

"You told me the first time it was you. Was it really you? At the time, I thought you told me you did, so I wouldn't blame myself after everything else that happened, and then, to Rick, you said I did it, so I got really confused. Adam, I won't be mad or upset; I am over it. I just need to know so I am not constantly wondering what happened to her." Wiping more tears from my eyes, he nodded.

"It wasn't planned, I swear."

"Maybe you can tell me what happened?"

"She came to see you that day, was going to tell you that she didn't want to marry me 'cause she knew how you felt about me..." He paused. "Well, how you felt about me back then. I came to stop her. When we got here, you were up in your room, sleeping. She wanted to wake you up, and I was trying to stop her. When she wouldn't listen, I decided to tie her up in the basement, at least till I could figure out what to do. I didn't know how long you were going to be up there. But I knew that the longer I left her there, the more chance you had of waking up, so I went back down. I was going to try to get her into the car and get her moved back into town, so we could talk about it some more. I was cutting the rope from the legs of the chair to move her, when she slammed the chair into me, attacking me, and I fell. When I finally got her off me, I saw that the knife had slit her throat. I don't know how, but it was in my hands and...anyway, you saw how she was."

"Yeah." More tears fell from my eyes.

"Emily, I'm sorry. I had hoped to move her before you saw, but you were moving around in your room and I didn't get the chance."

"Why did you tell Rick that I did it?"

"I was hoping it would get him to show you some compassion."

"Really? A girl murdering her sister is supposed to get him to feel sorry for me." I smiled, so did he.

"Okay, so in hindsight, maybe not the best thing to tell him."

"Adam, thank you for telling me," I said, and leaned in to give him a kiss. I would have preferred punching him or shoving him to the floor and stepping on him or kicking him, but not tonight. I was the sweet grieving wife who needs her husband to think he is in control and hopefully, I can form a plan to pay him back...somehow. I would not fall for any more of his lies. I would have to play his game, at least till I figured out how to get out of here. Maybe I could try leaving in the middle of the night when no one was awake. I went through the normal motions of the day, and sat at the table making more notes of what I was figuring out, details of the conversations that I heard from Rick and Adam. Also, since the journals were nowhere to be found, I tried to write down what I remembered. I hid the notes under the mattress in the spare bedroom, with the notes from before and then realized that if they were all in one spot, it would be easy to get rid of, so I split the notes up into different areas of the house.

At about two in the morning, I slipped out of bed and made my way downstairs. I grabbed the duffel bag I had hidden earlier that day and changed my clothes. I went to the music box and grabbed the car keys. So far so good. But as I tried to open the door, it wouldn't. The door wasn't locked, it just wouldn't open. I went to the window and tried to open it; it wouldn't budge.

"We've already gone over this, Emily. You can't leave." I turned around to see Adam standing at the bottom of the stairs. "So everything being cool with us was a lie?"

"Yeah, I guess it was, since I heard you and Rick talking last night." He had a momentary look of shock, before a sinister smile appeared on his face.

"Damn, was hoping that you would never find out about that, was hoping for things to remain more marital," he said with a smirk. "But it doesn't change the fact that you can't leave. This will just make things more uncomfortable for the next little while. Just don't do anything stupid and this can be relatively painless for you the next few months." So he was just playing nice for sex until he could kill me.

"All I have left is to do stupid things, Adam. And hope one of them works. Since I know you won't kill me till the babies are born." He widened his smile.

"It won't work. Nothing works. Everything you can think of has been tried."

"How do you know?"

"Because the original journal, the one passed down to the 12, details all the stupid things the women tried to do to stop this. Nothing has worked. The journals you have, my mom had. Those are nothing compared to the ones the men hand down."

"How can you be so cold?"

"Training. Rick made sure I knew the stakes. Emily, girls like you are great to have fun with, but far too inquisitive. Rick knew, that is why he wanted me to go after your sister, and it almost would have worked. But go figure, your sister's wild side and aloof attitude ended when I came to going through with it. I thought for sure, when I heard about her and James, it wouldn't be an issue, but seeing you get hurt over and over made it too real for her." By this time, he had made his way over to me.

"So not caring about anyone or anything is what you guys do. Use the women you marry to give you kids. Their feelings genuine, yours fake, until they decide to give up their lives. Have any of the women proved you wrong?"

"No, women care about the children too much. It is all part of the selection process to pick the caring, compassionate ones. My mom tried by telling my sister about the ritual first and hoping that it would end, but it didn't last, as you can see. We just had to be patient. Emily, just so you know, I really have enjoyed our time together. And we can make the next few months enjoyable too." Without thinking, I punched him, hard in the face. "I take it that is a no." He smirked, recovering quickly, rubbing his jaw. I stormed up the stairs and into the farthest guest bedroom, locking the door. I went to check the window, it opened. Duffel bag and keys meant leaving, the door and window downstairs wouldn't open. Second floor, no visible signs of leaving it open, or was it that there was something different about this room? I looked out the window, no ledges, nothing to climb down. I tore the sheets off the bed and tied them together. As I tried to throw it out the window, it slammed shut. So I couldn't prep anything. It wouldn't work. If I made it outside, it had to be with nothing. Come on, Emily, think. There had to be a way. I grabbed the chair by the desk and smashed the glass. The wood. It could only control the wood. I quickly threw the sheets out the window and making sure all the glass was out of the way, I started climbing down, only to have Adam's arm reach through the window and grab me.

"Let me go," I yelled, and struggled to pull my arm free from his grasp.

"Can't do that, Emily." I let go of the sheet and put my full weight on his arm, the sudden added weight caused him to scramble to hold onto the window frame. With his thoughts elsewhere, I lifted myself up and bit his hand. He released his grip just as I grabbed the sheet again and quickly lowered myself to the ground. I ran to the cover of the trees, knowing Adam would come looking for me. When I knew I was hidden, I tried to figure out a new plan. With Adam awake, it would be harder to get away and now that I was outside, if he caught me, he would make sure I couldn't get out again. I couldn't let him catch me. I heard footsteps; they were getting closer.

"You know, you keep surprising me, Emily. I wouldn't have expected any of this out of you. It is very stupid, but still surprising." Stupid. Why would it be stupid? I made it outside. I just needed to...I finally noticed. I couldn't move. The tree had wrapped its roots around my legs. So it wasn't just the house. It was the whole property. Anything of wood inside the property line was controlled by the ritual? By who? Emily, snap out of it, questions later, getting away now. I looked around for something to grab onto. There was a bush close by. I grabbed onto it and tried to pull myself free. Didn't work. I balled my hands into fists and tried to break the roots. They were too strong. Then, out of nowhere, they just let me go. I stood up just as Adam grabbed me and threw me over his shoulder and carried me back into the house. I kicked, scratched, and screamed at him the whole way back. He locked me in the bathroom. On the other side of the door, I heard him on the phone.

"Yeah, you were right. I am going to need the stuff, bring it as soon as you can." I checked the drawers and cupboards. The sleeping pills. I can give them to Adam and then get away. I saw a pair of scissors. I hesitated and decided not to right now. I just wanted to get away; I was not a murderer. Besides, the way my luck was going, I would probably stab myself with it. Wait, would that work? Threaten to kill myself before the kids are born if he didn't let me go? No, he wouldn't believe it. I wouldn't believe it and I am the one thinking about it. I don't know how long I was in there, maybe an hour, before I heard muffled sounds coming from outside the door. I heard strange sounds, like a chain dragging on the floor. After a few more minutes, the bathroom door opened. Adam grabbed me and restrained my arms behind my back. Rick followed him in with a shackle attached to a heavy chain. I tried to struggle to get free, but his grip tightened. I kicked Rick in the face, sending him reeling backward. But Adam's grip wouldn't lessen. I threw my head back, hitting him in the jaw. He scoffed.

"That only works once, Emily," he said, not loosening his grip. He forced me down to the floor, still keeping hold of my arms. He pressed his knee into my back. Rick now recovered, grabbed the shackle again, and managed to get it around my ankle.

"Adam," Rick said, and pointed to something. I turned my head just to see Adam pick up the bottle of pills. They must have fallen out of my pocket in the struggle.

"Well, you surprised me yet again, Emily. Too bad I can't keep you. Life with you would be so much fun," he said, releasing my other arm and standing up. "Word of warning, Emily—"

"Warning, my life is over as soon as the babies are born. There is no need to warn me about anything," I said.

"Suit yourself. Rick." Adam and Rick went outside. I exited the bathroom. Looks like I had enough chain to reach the kitchen, living room, and the first guest bedroom upstairs, not the second one. It would let me get a little way off the porch, but not a lot further than that. I sat down on the couch and brought my knees up to my chest while watching the fire in the fireplace. Adam came in a while later and watched me for a bit. His eyes were cold, empty. How could he have made such a fool out of me? Tears welled up in my eyes. I couldn't believe what an idiot I've been. It happened with James and I forgave him. Adam, same thing. I keep acting so stupid around men. Why couldn't I have met anyone decent, who actually cared about me? Tears started rolling down my cheeks. Adam started to move closer to me.

"Don't you dare," I said, glaring at him. He returned to his seat. For a brief moment, I thought I saw an emotion in his eyes, but it was gone so quickly. It could have been me imagining it, maybe hoping for a sliver of humanity, something to remind me of the Adam he was before. I laid down on the couch and pulled the blanket over me, continuing to watch the fire.

I woke up sometime during the night and realized I was hungry; I hadn't eaten much today. I made my way to the kitchen, the chain dragging along the floor woke Adam from sleep in the chair. He followed me into the kitchen and watched as I made a sandwich.

"How many times have the women made you guys resort to this method?" I said, swinging my leg back and forth to make the chain move along the floor.

"Seven, including you," he said.

"Let me guess, they all needed to be taken care of afterward too." He looked at me.

"Yes."

"So how do you plan to take care of me?" I said, looking him straight in the eyes, as I took a bite of my sandwich. There it was again, for a brief second, I saw. Was I getting to him?

"Any preference?" he said coldly.

"You're giving me a choice?" he shrugged.

"Not really a choice, more like curious."

"I asked you first. How would you have killed me if I wouldn't have found out about it?"

"Probably overdose."

"Coward," I said boldly. He looked taken aback by my response.

"Why, it's what you were going to do to me, isn't it?" he said, pulling the pills out of his shirt pocket.

"No, I was going to put you to sleep so I could get away. I am not a killer." I emphasized the last word so he knew that I would mean him.

"It was never meant to be this way, Emily."

"I know the spirits messed up your plans. I'm surprised you haven't done anything about them since they have caused you such an inconvenience."

"We don't know how. They showed up randomly and we never knew about the other journal." I smirked and started to laugh. I got up and put my empty plate by the sink and grabbed a glass of water.

"Wow, you guys don't know that part? All your years of studying for all these generations which, by the way, nice work telling everyone that these cabins are only a few generations old. When, in reality, they are a lot older."

"What part?" he asked, ignoring the rest of what I said.

"Why the spirits only come out sometimes? Who the spirits are? It is not random," I said, and made my way past him to the living room.

"Then why?" he said, trailing after me.

"Nope, you are getting nothing more out of me." I laid back down on the couch and ignored his questions till he got frustrated and gave up.

Chapter 15

A few days later, after Adam realized I wouldn't talk to him anymore, he stopped asking. The doctor and Rick showed up. Adam wanted the doctor to make sure everything was fine with the babies with everything that has happened.

"She's lying, Adam. She knows nothing," Rick said, raising his voice. I smiled. The doctor, from looking at them to looking at me.

"Is it true? Do you know why?"

"I do," I said confidently.

"And you won't tell them?"

"Why should I? The spirits are here to help cause you guys trouble. If I tell you, then you might find a way to get rid of them, and they are trying to help people like me." They were all looking at me now. "By the way, Ray will now be joining the spirits in this place," I said, looking pointedly at Adam. "Just thought you should know," I said, smiling more when I saw the look on his face. I couldn't help but laugh.

"Adam, go, I'll watch her for a bit," Rick said. Adam stormed out of the house and I heard the tires screech as he peeled down the road. The doctor backed off and Rick grabbed me. "Just because we can't kill you yet doesn't mean we can't hurt you," he said, smiling. I looked from him to the doctor, who looked like he was going to allow Rick to do what he wanted. I didn't let him see my fear. I didn't know how bad he meant to hurt me, but it wouldn't be anything good. After all, it was his guidance that turned Adam into what he is.

"Go ahead then," I said firmly. I didn't move; I didn't cower as he raised his hand.

"Don't worry, I'll start off easy, and you can stop this anytime, you just need to tell me what you know."

"Quit stalling and get it over with, I am not saying a word."

A lot of time passed, but I didn't know how much. I hurt everywhere. I was bleeding everywhere.

"Rick, seriously," Adam said, coming in the door. "She is pregnant, you didn't have to go that far." Adam rushed to my side, trying to help me up. I pushed him away.

"I don't need your help. Go on, Rick," I said, turning my attention back to him. He stabbed the knife into my leg again. I muffled the scream, though it rang loud and clear in my head.

"Rick, enough." Adam glared at him. The doctor came to check on me again.

"She is not going to last much longer. If it keeps going, the babies will be in danger. You need to end this quickly, or stop right now if you don't think she will talk."

"Or he could just end all this now, killing me and the kids, 'cause I want no part of this. Adam can find himself a new wife now that his life is no longer in danger. Oh, no, wait, you don't do the killing, do you, Rick? You train Adam to be heartless and do it for you."

"Emily, stop."

"Why, I am dead anyway," I yelled. "No matter what I do, I am dead. Currently, my only option seems to be to take my children with me, so you can't use them in your twisted games."

"Emily, you can't mean that," Adam said, looking worried. I turned back to Rick.

"Go ahead, Rick, I dare you." The look of determination on my face said it all. He knew I was goading him into killing me. He dropped the knife at my feet. The doctor moved in and started patching me up. Although none of the wounds were life threatening, I still needed stitches. My eye was swollen shut; I had cuts and bruises everywhere but my stomach.

"You went too far, Rick. If she was going to talk, she would have done it a long time ago. You need to leave. Now."

"Are you going soft on me, Adam?"

"No, but for the next few months, until it is time, she is still carrying my children." Rick left. "And you, why would you let him go that far?" he said, turning to the doctor.

"As long as the babies are safe, it is not for me to question Rick." He finished patching me up and headed for the door. "I'll come check on her tomorrow."

"I'll get you come clean clothes," Adam said, and went upstairs. I headed to the bathroom and hopped in the shower. The cuts stung as the water hit them, but was nothing compared to what Rick put me through. The only thing that kept me going was knowing he was frustrated at my lack of screams and annoyed at my silence.

"Emily, I—" Adam said, standing in the doorway.

"Come to check on your uncle's artwork," I said, interrupting him. I stood in front of him naked, letting him see every cut, every bruise. He handed me the clothes and turned away.

"You could have ended it. It was your choice to not tell him. It was stupid of you to not just tell him what he wanted to know." I finished getting dressed and pushed past him.

"I told you before, Adam, all I have left is stupid. I have till they are born," I said, putting my hand on my stomach. "I have a few months to figure out how I can survive, how to get my babies out of here so they don't have to go through this." I turned to look at him and added. "And I have to do this all alone, so doing things that might be stupid to you are the only things I have left. If I stop trying, I might as well end my life myself."

"Emily, you can't," he said, panicked.

"First of all, I can do anything I want, I'm already dead. Second, you can no longer tell me what you do. I think that you wanting to murder me nullifies the wedding vows of me obeying you." I turned and went to the kitchen to make myself something to eat. Out of the corner of my eye, I saw the pained look on Adam's face. It was a while before he came into the kitchen to check on me.

He sat down at the table across from me.

"So how many of the seven did you have to resort to beating the shit out of?" I asked.

"No others," he said.

"Good, it seems Rick enjoys himself too much, would hate for him to get to do it too often."

"He's not—" I raised my eyebrow to look at him.

"If you are going to tell me he is not that bad, can you honestly look at what he did to me, or to you for that matter and say he is not that bad."

"Me? He didn't do anything to me."

"He turned you into a heartless, manipulative asshole, and you say he didn't do anything to you. I feel sorry for your mom, giving her life to save someone like you." I could tell my words hurt him. I stormed out of the kitchen and paused when I got to the spot that was covered with my blood. Something was happening. I knelt down on the ground.

"Adam, is this normal?" I called to the kitchen. Adam appeared beside me and watched the blood with me.

"I have never seen this before." We watched as the blood soaked into the wood of the floor. But not only was it being soaked, more like being drank. It was slow, and as the blood got soaked into the wood, it turned back to the normal color, as if it had never happened. The knife was still on the floor. I grabbed it quickly and cut a gash in Adam's hand.

"What the hell, Emily?" I dropped the knife and he bent to pick it up. As the blood dripped off his hand and onto the floor, it did nothing. It stayed in the drops where they fell. He watched with me. "What…"

"No idea, maybe you need to have a talk with the other 11 families," I said, getting up, and sat in front of the fireplace. That was weird, it had never happened before. Not with James's blood, not with Ben's, not with Raylene's. Why now, why mine? And why not Adam's? Or did it have anything to do with it being mine at all? This was really confusing. After realizing that it wouldn't do the same thing to his blood, he cleaned it up and bandaged up his hand. I added a couple logs to the fire and laid down on the couch. I didn't sleep much that night. Every time I moved; I was in pain. I don't think Adam slept much either, my crying out when I moved kept waking him up. He didn't say anything.

I slept or half slept till almost noon the next day. I got up when the doctor knocked on the door. He checked me over and went to talk to Adam upstairs to make sure I wouldn't overhear. More than likely, he was telling him about what happened with my blood. I was cleaning up the kitchen when they came back down.

"I am sorry. I can't give you anything, Emily, but try to rest."

"You guys really need to stop telling me what to do, both of you let this happen," I said, annoyed, not looking at either of them.

"Right, well, Adam, she seems fine—" I interrupted him.

"Fine, I am not fine," I yelled. "Rick may not have crossed the line or the house would have stopped him, but I am not fine."

"The house wouldn't have done anything to Rick even if he had," the doctor said.

"Yes, it would. The ritual contract was between me and Adam. If my life was threatened beyond that of torture or that of the babies, the house would have taken him out."

"So that was your plan? Push him to doing something stupid so the house would have no choice?" Adam looked impressed.

"You came back too early and ruined it. So, your uncle owes you his life; at the very least, a thank you. I might not have long, but I am not rolling over without a fight, and if I can take any of you with me, I will. So, you all might want to watch your back around me from now on," I said, smiling sweetly.

"I thought you said you are not a killer?"

"I'm not, doesn't mean I won't get the house to do it for me."

They walked outside, talking more, while I searched the kitchen for something to pick the lock with. I found two skewers and carefully placed them under the cushions of the couch when Adam walked in the house. I quickly sat down before he noticed me. That night, as he lay sleeping on the chair, I pulled the skewer out and started trying to pick the lock. I guess I was being noisier than I thought, because I noticed Adam watching me intently.

"Emily, stop, it is pointless."

"No," I stated, and kept trying.

"You are not making this easy."

"Good." I saw a small hint of a smile, as Adam shook his head.

"I can't understand you; I never would have imagined it would be this way." I looked at him.

"What way?"

"That I would…that I would feel…Emily, I respect your fight. It is stupid, and you won't win, but I respect it." I turned away and continued working on the lock. Adam watched me, highly amused, as I worked the lock with the skewers. After a little more prodding and wiggling, the lock snapped open. Adam rushed over and grabbed the skewers and locked the shackle again. He also went to the kitchen and cleared out anything that was small enough to allow me to pick the lock. He took them all upstairs into the last bedroom, knowing that I couldn't reach it. He did a thorough job in the kitchen; nothing was small enough. Over the next couple days, while Adam was at work, he had the doctor and Rick stay outside the house, watching to make sure that I didn't get out. With instructions to the doctor to make sure Rick was not allowed near me. As all this was going on, I was making my own journal. I wrote down everything that was happening, everything I was thinking might work, any plans that I was going to try, and tomorrow, I would try another one, provided I could get enough time alone. Slowly, each of the men from the families started stopping by to make sure what Adam told them about my blood was true and each time the look of shock on their faces showed that this had never happened before.

Chapter 16

After Adam left for work, I watched as Rick's truck pulled into the driveway. He made no attempt to get out. I locked the front door, and drew the curtains closed. I stuck the fireplace poker in the fire while I went to go make some breakfast. After eating, I returned to the fireplace and sat in front of the fire. I grabbed the poker, held it in the loop of one of the chain links. It was very slow, but I was making progress. As I was trying to speed up the process by stretching the loop with the poker, it slipped and hit my skin. I was about to cry out when I heard the door handle wiggle. I quickly put the poker back on the stand and climbed on the couch, pulling the blanket over me, covering the shackle. I closed my eyes and pretended to sleep. I heard the key go into the lock and the door opening. I made sure not to jump, not to open my eyes. Let him think I was sleeping. I could feel eyes watching me, was it Rick? My heart was starting to beat faster. I heard no footsteps walking any direction. Was he just watching me? Creep much. After what seemed like forever, I heard the footsteps going outside and the door close. I waited a little longer, the door did not lock again, but I heard the footsteps leave the porch. I opened my eyes, slowly breathing a sigh of relief. I tried not to think about Rick watching me. I made my way to the window and slowly moved the curtain a bit, Rick was on the phone, standing back at his truck. I locked the door again and tried to work on the chain some more. After lunch, I rubbed cream on the blistering part of my ankle and worked on more notes. If I wasn't going to be here for my children, I was going to leave them details, as much as I could figure out, before Adam decided it would be time for me to go.

"All right, Ray, I am going to need your help just in case I can't get out of here. I will need you to lead my children to these, just like the others did for me. I am not giving up. This is the only worst-case scenario here," I said out loud, hoping, maybe praying, that she would hear me. I hid the new papers in the fake drawer in the china cabinet. More places I hide stuff, more chances that some of the notes would remain. In all my notes I was writing, I made sure not to write why the spirits of the two were hanging around, why they were choosing to help, just in case Adam found them. I couldn't have him finding out. It was kind of lonely in the house, knowing the spirits would not be popping out to help me anymore. Knowing they couldn't, even if they wanted to. I would have loved to hear Raylene's voice again. I would have loved to talk to her and find out exactly what happened, if what Adam told me was true. I wanted to tell her how sorry I was, it wasn't supposed to be her. Adam would be home soon, I quickly made a sandwich and sat down on the couch, covering the shackle again. I would have to try to work on it some more tonight or tomorrow when Adam went to work.

When Adam got home, he looked around like he was surveying if anything was moved or different.

"Why did you lock the door?" he asked.

"I watched Rick pull up when you left. Without the doctor this time. It was for protection. After what he did last time, I didn't want him in here," I replied. Adam nodded.

"Don't do it again."

"Why not? You gave him a key; he came in here anyway."

"Yeah, and how would you know that?"

"Because I only pretended to be sleeping, Adam. Do you seriously think I could sleep knowing a guy like him was around? After what he did to me? You trusted him to not touch me again? I hoped that by pretending to be asleep, he would leave me alone."

"Well, he is the only one I trust."

"Really, after what he did to me, you trust him. Even you thought he went too far." He avoided looking at me directly.

"He didn't hurt you…again. You are fine."

"And if I had been awake? What would he have done then?"

"I am done talking about this."

"Fine." I laid down on the couch and ignored him for the rest of the night. I didn't care that he tried to talk to me; I barely heard him when he asked if I had thought about baby names. I stared at him. He was seriously asking me what I wanted to name my kids, knowing I would not be there for them.

"I just wanted your opinion. You are their mother after all."

"That is cold, even for you. Knowing what you plan to do to me and asking my opinion." A sudden look of guilt flashed across his eyes. I wanted to believe I was making progress in changing his mind about killing me. But thinking back to how many times I have been gullible enough to believe him, to be sucked in by his stories. I turned away from him, as a tear fell down my cheek. Adam got up and went to get some dinner. Think, Emily, you can figure this out, you can get away. You can save them; you can be with them. You can watch them grow up. Just get yourself out of this.

"Why are you sleeping down here instead of in your bed?" Adam asked me later that night. "You have been sleeping down here for days, wouldn't your bed be more comfortable?"

"Because in that room, you were different, you were the man I was hoping to spend the rest of my life with. And that is the way I will remember it. I do not want to be in that room, with you watching me the way you are now. You are not the person I grew up with, you are not the man I thought you were. You are a monster," I choked out the last few words, and then, was silent. There was a lump in my throat, it hurt. I wanted to say so much more. I wanted so much to scream at him, to cry. But I couldn't, I couldn't give him the satisfaction. I couldn't help but wonder if all of them had a club, where they would discuss the latest tantrum or sob-fest that the women in their lives were putting them through. But what if I could get through to him? Would it be worth it to try? No. It wasn't, any common decency had been pushed out of him long ago. Only the actor pretending to be a kind man was left. Until he got what he wanted. Until I foolishly fell for all his lies. He didn't reply to my statements, he left the room instead.

A little while later, he came out of the washroom. He had just gotten out of the shower. Beads of water dripped off his hair and onto his bare chest. After everything he put me through, how could I…I hated myself for still being attracted to him. He caught me staring at him and I turned away. I guess that was what made him so good with his deception. Even if he only pretended to be sweet, his looks were not fake in any way. He was the kind of man that every woman at first glance would want. And only someone as stupid as me would still find a guy like him attractive, even knowing what he was.

"I won't refuse if you wanted to have some fun," he said smugly.

"I don't, I…" I forced myself not to look at him.

"Sure you do."

"I am in enough pain, thank you very much. I don't need to add more to my life right now."

"I am sure I could make you feel something other than pain."

"No, you couldn't, because looking at you keeps reminding me of the pain of my bad judgment. The pain of me being so gullible, to fall for you, when I should have known better. The pain of everything that you will allow to happen to our kids." I didn't have to look at him to know that he was no longer smirking. He left the room. When he came back, he was dressed, he sat in the chair, watching me. He didn't say anything. I closed my eyes. I couldn't look at him watching me. A couple of hours later, I slowly took the blanket and carefully started wrapping it around the chain so it would not make noise as it moved across the floor. I sat in front of the fireplace again and worked at the chain link quietly so I wouldn't wake Adam. When I finally got it burned through, I quietly stood up. I was free, but I hadn't planned anything. I couldn't remember where I left the car keys, more than likely I dropped them upstairs the day Adam caught me climbing out the window. I quietly climbed the stairs and checked the floor of the room. The room was cold, it had the fall leaves blowing into the room off the trees. Adam hadn't been in here to fix the window. I rummaged through the items from the kitchen that he brought up here and grabbed the two skewers. I grabbed the pillow case and tore off a couple strips. Taking off my pants, I tied the skewers to my leg. I put my pants back on and saw the keys under the dresser. Yes, finally something was going my way. Okay, so can't touch the wood. I put the car keys in my pocket and spread the blanket out and wrapped it around my body. I looked around the room. So, the house had eyes to help it see. Because so far, nothing I had done had been stopped, and something in this room, or lack of something, was preventing it from seeing. Emily, stop, you are almost free, stop thinking about it. I pulled myself together. Calm down, Emily. I took a deep breath and started again climbing down the bed-sheet rope. I was almost at the bottom when I saw Adam waiting at the bottom for me. He had woken up. I silenced my frustration. Why couldn't anything be easy, hadn't I suffered enough? Okay, Emily, think. If I get to the bottom, Adam will definitely grab me. My best option was to try and climb back up. Hide out in the room till I could come up with a new plan. I started climbing back up. My arms were burning, but I couldn't give up now.

"Come on, Emily, just climb down and we can get this over with. You know you are not going anywhere. Just give up now."

I ignored him.

"By the way, clever plan melting the chain."

I still ignored him. I wouldn't make it back to the top. I lowered myself a little bit.

"See this is much easier, just let me take you back inside."

I took a deep breath and loosened the blanket that was wrapped around me, dropping it, making sure to cover Adam's face. I released my grip on the bed sheet and fell on him. Not expecting any of that, Adam fell to his knees. He was momentarily caught off guard, but still able to move. I lifted myself off of him, and before he could get himself untangled, I tied the bed sheet around the blanket as tight as I could and ran. As I reached the front of the house, I saw Rick's truck pull up. Shit. Adam must have called him when he woke up and noticed the chain.

I couldn't let myself be caught, but I didn't know what to do. If I ran back to the back of the house, Adam was there, in front of me was Rick, and everywhere else were the trees. I crouched down and waited. I knew I couldn't wait long. Think, Emily. I grabbed the car keys out of my pocket and stuck the key through the gap in my fingers, closing my fist around it. Not the most ideal weapon, but convenient.

"Emily, you can't get away," I heard Adam's voice, getting closer. Damn it, I waited too long, Adam had gotten himself free. I couldn't take on both of them. I would have to run for the car now or lose my chance completely. I bolted out of my hiding place and ran. I made it halfway to the car when it grabbed me and lifted me off the ground. I turned around to see the railings of the porch stretched all the way to me and wrapped around my waist. I struggled to get free, but it gripped me tighter. I threw the car keys and watched them land near the car, maybe I will have another chance and get a little closer next time.

"You won't get out of here, Emily. I am sorry, but that is just the way it is," Adam said, coming up behind me.

"I guess I should thank you, Adam, I would have never realized what I am capable of without you. I thought I was just supposed to be a wife. That pleasing James or you was all that I was supposed to do. I won't quit trying to get away. The minute I stop trying is when you should worry about me." He unlocked the shackle that was around my ankle and attached the new one that Adam had asked Rick to bring.

"Ready?" Rick asked Adam. Adam nodded. As Adam grabbed my arms, my waist was released and the porch railing went back to how it was before. I didn't struggle much between Adam having my wrists secure and the shackle on my ankle Rick was holding the chain, for I knew I wouldn't get anywhere. After securing the new chain, Adam looked around, moved all the fireplace tools upstairs into the bedroom I couldn't reach. Damn it. Adam returned a little while later. I stood up and went to the washroom to get cleaned up. I had to be careful since I couldn't fully close the door. I turned on the shower and carefully untied the skewers from my leg, hiding them in the cabinet. Since he was awake and probably wouldn't be going back to sleep any time soon, there was no need for me to try again tonight. Also, even if I did, I wouldn't get very far; I was exhausted.

"I admit this is a first. The previous women never thought of that."

"I'm happy for you, now you get to add something to the book. Something new that your stupid wife tried and didn't get away with." It looked like he wanted to say something, but decided not to.

"How are you okay with all of this? Did you know about what the cabin could do?"

"Yes." He looked at me.

"And you are okay with all of it?"

"Why wouldn't I be?"

"Something is alive in this cabin, controlling the wood, keeping you captive, and you are okay with all of it. Do you even know who or what it is?"

"I am not the one that is captive, you are."

"Literally, maybe I am, but so are you. You started the ritual with me, which means it has you too. Whatever it wanted me for, you are a part of." He didn't reply. I went to sleep.

The next day, I expected Adam to go to work and have Rick parked outside again. He didn't. He stayed watching me all day. I would have to try a new plan when he went to sleep.

"Doctor called and wanted me to check out how you are healing, do you mind?" he said, after getting off the phone. I shook my head. He checked, cleaned, and re-bandaged the wounds on my leg and arms. When he attempted to do the ones on my face, I backed away.

"I can do these ones myself." He stared into my eyes and I looked away, he backed off. I went to the washroom and cleaned the wounds on my face.

"So why bother with all of this?"

"Depends on what you are talking about."

"Why not just lock me in the secret room, then you wouldn't have to worry about me trying to escape."

"Can't."

"Why?" I asked, curious.

"No wood down there."

"So, there is also no way out of there, would be a lot less headache for you."

"You don't need to understand, and I don't expect you to, but I can't."

It was two more days before he went back to work. I asked him if he could bring me a few books; I was getting bored having nothing to do. He didn't answer me. I guess I would just have to wait and see if he would actually do it. It didn't matter, today was my day to try again. I went to the bathroom and looked in the cabinet, the skewers were gone. Shit. I went to the kitchen and grabbed cooking oil, drenching the shackle and my ankle and tried pulling it off. No luck. I was still working away at it when Adam found me in the kitchen. He had come home early to check on me.

"Emily, stop, please," he said, looking at my ankle still bleeding with the skin peeling off from my trying to force it off.

"No."

"You are going to hurt yourself."

I started laughing. "You mean, more than Rick already has? Trust me, that is not possible unless I cut off my foot."

"Would you?" he asked, concerned.

"Don't know yet. The doctor told Rick not to when he asked if he could. He said the stress of limb loss, as well as blood loss, would be really hard on the babies."

"Then you shouldn't even consider it."

"Adam, I have told you before, quit trying to tell me what to do. If you were concerned for your kids, you would let me go. You would let me raise them away from here, no matter what it cost you. That is what you would do, if you cared. You would not make them go through this." He stormed outside. I couldn't tell if I was getting through to him. Or not. But my gut was telling me I wasn't. He was trying to make me think he was changing just to get me to stop. I was getting tired. I laid down on the couch and was fast asleep in no time. I didn't hear when Adam came back inside. I didn't wake up when he bandaged up my ankle.

Over the next couple of weeks, Adam had Rick take over for him at work and stayed home, watching over me like a hawk. There were days I actually tried to escape and other days when I sat on the couch thinking of how to escape. But each time, Adam was right there to stop me. Even when I tried to hide what I was doing, he caught me. The chain would give me away, or the one time I almost made it by trying to undo the screws that were holding the chain to the wall, I was on the last screw when the floorboards started to move. Almost like a tornado was moving under the house and lifting each board up and down. They reached Adam and woke him up. After he realized what was happening, the floor stopped moving, and again, I was stopped. I wanted the spirits to come back and help. I was tired of feeling so alone. I had to keep believing I could get out. When he woke up, I was staring at him.

"What's wrong?"

"You mean, besides everything?"

"Emily, come on, you are making this a lot harder than it needs to be."

"For whom, you? Good, that is the plan. There is no reason that I should be the only one who is suffering." He sighed.

"I guess I should be grateful that you are talking to me again?"

"I guess that depends, on whether you actually want me to be talking. If you don't, then I guess no."

"You are impossible. I do not know if I should be amused or not that you haven't given up your escape attempts. That you still try and defy everything I ask of you. That you will not listen to a word I say about you not being able to get away. So what new plans have you concocted by staring at me?"

"I am wondering if it would be easier to get away if I kill you," I said, casually watching his reaction. "There are many ways I could, lots of knives in the kitchen. Hitting you over the head with a lamp." He watched me intently as I spoke, maybe trying to gauge if I was serious, if I had finally gotten to the point that I could kill someone. I wondered if it was the right thing to do. Letting him know that I was thinking of ways to kill him might not have been the best plan. He would need to make sure he was the one still in control. And a couple days later, to prove his point, he shortened the chain so that it would only reach to the front door and the bathroom. That I could no longer reach the kitchen and I could no longer go into any of the bedrooms upstairs. Maybe I actually made him nervous talking about knives in the kitchen.

Since he shortened it, he now served me all my meals. Made sure I sat by the door for a couple of hours a day to get some fresh air. And finally brought me a few books. I think it was more for his benefit than it was for mine. He was getting pretty bored too. I was running out of ideas, and time. Over the next few days, my appetite decreased, so did my attempts to escape. I sat staring at the fire most of my days now. I would catch Adam staring at me more each day, with what almost looked like concern. When I noticed them, I kept trying to see if he had changed back, back to the Adam that I knew before. I so wanted him to be who he was before. But each time, his answers told me he was long gone.

When Adam was upstairs one day, grabbing me clean clothes, I finally decided I had had enough. I was tired. I grabbed all the supplies from the bathroom cupboard that were labeled flammable and hid them behind the couch cushions. It was another two days of thinking about my plan; I didn't want to do it. But what choice did I have? Everything I tried, Adam stopped. And if I ever got close, it was the house that stopped me. From moving the floorboards to wrapping the bannister around my wrists till Adam could re-secure the shackle or anything else that I may have messed up.

A few days more and I had my chance. Adam went to take a shower; it was time. I put my hand on my stomach and whispered a prayer of apology. With tears streaming down my face, I emptied the flammable chemicals around the room all around me. I grabbed a piece of kindling and lit it on fire from the fireplace. I stood by the couch and lit the cushions on fire, then the curtains, and walked to the center of the room as Adam came out of the bathroom. I dropped the wood and stared at Adam. I watched the look of horror on his face as the room ignited on fire, spreading quickly from the accelerant.

"Emily," he yelled, but couldn't get to me. The flames had engulfed the room. My clothes had caught on fire. I felt the searing heat on my flesh. I collapsed to the ground, no longer able to stand, my skin burning. I closed my eyes. Adam watched, unable to do anything. I screamed as the flames devoured me. He started coughing and with one last look at me, shut the bathroom door.

Chapter 17

I was alive? The pain was lessening. How? I opened my eyes. The cabin was…The flames were being put out? I watched as the flames lessened, like they were being smothered. The scorched floor was repairing. The cabin, like the music box, would not burn. How could I be alive?

I tried to pick myself off the floor. I couldn't move.

"Emily, that was really stupid," Adam said, coming into my view. I couldn't speak. He said nothing further to me, a little while later, the doctor showed up and examined me. After a few minutes, he finally spoke.

"We can't move her; you will have to leave her here. If she loses contact with the house, her body will die. The house will keep the babies safe inside her till it is time." Inside, I cried. I hoped to spare my children from this and instead, I did nothing. They would still be born. I am sorry.

"I told you, you wouldn't get away. I told you that you were mine," I heard a voice say. *Who?*

"I am what you were trying to find out about. What you called the cabin?" *You can understand me?* I thought.

"Of course, you are one with me now. I have you. I own you. I won. No one ever beats me. I must say, Adam was right about you, you certainly were impressive. Much more than I thought you would be." *Why?*

"Perhaps, for now, you should contemplate what you have done. How you have accomplished nothing. We will have plenty of time to talk. For your actions, I have decided this will be your punishment. You will watch everything. I could have easily made it that you wouldn't have, but this will make it more fun." Whoever this was, was worse than Adam. So much worse. The voice stopped talking to me.

I watched Adam come and go, the doctor would come once a week to check on me. Occasionally, Adam would stop and look at me, maybe say a few words of disappointment that I would try to kill the babies. But he left me no other choice. What choice did I have? I tried everything I could. Even if what I did was wrong, if it saved future generations pain, wouldn't it be worth it? Either way, I guess it didn't matter in the end anyway. I solved nothing by doing this.

One particularly emotional day for Adam, might have had a bad day at work, he actually sat down to talk to me. Did he know that I was still here? Or was it more just so he would have someone to talk to.

I was crying, screaming, yelling. But outwardly, my body didn't move. I couldn't scream. My body burnt beyond recognition was no longer my body, just a vessel that was carrying the next generation of victims for this cabin. The cabin…that has spilled so much blood. Is this what was intended in the beginning. Is this what they wanted? Every time I screamed or yelled inside; I would hear the voice laugh. But it did not speak to me. He was enjoying this.

The days dragged into months, until the day for me to give birth finally came. I watched as the doctor grabbed his scalpel. I was awaiting the pain that didn't come. Right, the cabin's incubator, my body was only a vessel, how could it feel pain? The only pain I would feel was from my thoughts of not being able to stop this. I barely got to hear their cry before the eyes of this body went dim.

But as those eyes closed, I saw something new. I saw the reflections of all those that had come before. In the grandfather clock, in the dining table. I felt their energy. Only in the main floor of the cabin, and my bedroom, nothing in the guest rooms. The items made to start the ritual. They trapped us here, held our souls when we died. They used our energy, our eyes, our ears. That was how the house knew. It was all the people that had died before that protected the cabin, that kept it alive, that would not let the ritual fail. That now I…would not be allowed to let fail.

"Emily," the voice finally spoke to me again. I watched my family's faces reflected in the items scattered around the room, as they heard the voice too. This was new, this was different. The look of shock on their faces told me so.

What? I asked.

"It is almost time."

For what?

"For why I wanted you. For why it had to be you. It is time for you to fulfill the contract. For why I needed you. Granted this was not exactly what I had planned, you chose to change things, and it is what you left me to work with."

"I will do nothing to help you."

"You will, in time. Here, time means nothing. You will help me," the voice said with an eerie laugh, and for now, he left me alone with the thoughts. He needed me?

This was the suffering I had to endure. To watch their lives and not be a part of it. I wondered if Adam would also join me, trapped in this music box when he died. Would he think all this was worth it? Or would he finally agree that the price of blood was too high? I would spend each year watching my children grow, watching them play, watching them fight. Watching Adam as he chose one to live and one to die. And I cried.